Book 2

Sequel to Treacherous Desires

Desires REVISITED

KRITIKA SHARMA

BOOKS BY KRITIKA SHARMA

FICTION:

Desires Series
Treacherous Desires (Book 1)
Desires Revisited (Book 2)

Ghost Series
Live-in with a Ghost (Book 1)
In Love with a Ghost (Book 2)
Forever with a Ghost (Book 3)

Jab We Quarantined (Short Read)
Be My Quarantine (Short Read)

The Slut Chronicles Series:
Betrayed (Book 1)
Enslaved (Book 2)
Obsessed (Book 3)

The Rogue Spy – The Delhi Chapter (Book 1)

Perfect Crimes Series:
The Girl Who Died: Perfect Crimes Episode 1
The Stolen Diamonds: Perfect Crimes Episode 2
The Silent Death: Perfect Crimes Episode 3

NON-FICTION:

Manage your Manager

Know more about her works at:
www.kritikasharma.in

Desires REVISITED

KRITIKA SHARMA

KALAMOS LITERARY SERVICES LLP

Kalamos Literary Services LLP
Email: info@kalamos.co.in
First Published in 2023
by
Kalamos Literary Services

ISBN - 978-93-91142-47-6

Desires Revisited
Kritika Sharma

Cover designed and typeset in Kalamos Literary Services LLP

For my husband, Rajat

For my Sun and the Moon and all my stars, i.e. my beautiful children, Vihaan and Vanya

And for my dearest friend, Anuj

Thank you to all of you.

Prologue

Life takes all kinds of turns and mine took a major swerve when I met the man of my dreams in an office party around 10 months ago.

Shaun Malani is the owner of one of the biggest multinational conglomerate of the world, and somehow, unintentionally, shockingly, he fell head over heels in love with me.

I was already married at the time, but truth be told it was a very unhappy marriage, my life was a complete mess. Then a trip to Australia sparked something between us, Shaun and me. But I still maintained my distance and tried to salvage my marriage, well as much as I could.

However, release of some compromising photos pushed my marriage to the point of no return and I found myself in the arms of the man I was avoiding and yet was craving so much.

One thing led to another, and the guilt of cheating on my then husband, despite the situation, overtook me and I stabbed myself fatally.

Shaun saved me in the nick of time, and our relationship was announced to the world.

Now, engaged and together for four months, I am seriously looking forward to living my happily ever after with the man I so madly and deeply love.

Now, finally, I am going to live with my Shaun in London.

Chapter 1

London

As I stepped inside the office premises, every head turned in my direction.

I sighed as I observed the same process. It was now very common. It didn't matter where I went, when I went, and whom I talked to, I was the gossip of the town. Even my friends were under the radar now. Simi was my best friend in the world, and there was no newspaper or magazine whose journalist had not hounded her recently. Same was the situation for my parents and brother, Arsh. And Daksh, oh my ex-husband Daksh! He had to drop off the grid for a while to get away from the heat and media splash. The journalists had bothered him shamelessly, but given the gentleman that he is, instead of dishing all bad stuff about me, he had decided to take a long vacay and go to the mountains with some friends.

Yes, things were ugly for a while but it did result in one good thing. Seeing all the drama around and how much it was affecting me mentally, emotionally and physically, my father – despite my mother's non-stop tantrums – had given me his reluctant blessing to fly out to London and live a quiet life. Or as quiet my life could get.

So yeah! Now here I was… in the big foreign city, full of people who either hated me or were jealous of me… but hey, I feel I would eventually grow fond of this place, after all, I have to spend my entire life here now.

As I walked inside the big office, the headquarters of the Malani Group, I realized how magnificent it was, just like everyone had described. The walls were painted in various shades of soothing colours with many informative flyers hanging from the ceiling. The open plan office had desks and chairs sprawled across the floor and there was an aura of elegance reflecting from every corner. I was deeply impressed by this office. There was something in the surrounding that resonated the word 'Spectacular'. It was prestigious and suited the name it represented. I stared around as I made my way inside and caught my own reflection in the opposite glass wall and for a second I could not recognize myself. I was wearing a white knee-length dress, white pencil heels with white elegant accessories. A stunning white bag was dangling from my left hand, while the right hand held a black folder and my phone. As if on cue, my phone buzzed and I looked down.

I hope you are just about to arrive ... Can't wait to meet you.

I smiled at the message, and then looked around to find a spot to make myself comfortable. I had called him the moment I had landed but he had been entering a board meeting at that time.

"I will see you the moment you arrive here, okay?" his happiness was audible in his voice. "And I am so sorry for not being able to pick you up," he apologized.

"I know," I replied. "See you very soon," I smiled too.

"Sooner."

Yes, I had promised him that I will let him know the moment I would arrive at the office, but Nadine, his assistant, had informed me that there was some fire and he was busy putting it out in the board meeting. And that's why I had deliberately not informed him now that I was already here, for I knew he would have left the meeting and rushed over to meet!

I smiled at his cuteness and looked around, only to be shocked. Girls, white and mostly blonde, were eyeing me with intimidation. Many were shuffling from one seat to another whispering; were they wondering who the hell I was! Boys too were eyeing me and I could see their grins and nudges to point at me. Only if *he* was with me, all would have been silenced. And soon it would be.

I had flown down to London only this morning but I had wanted to be here right away. I had changed in the restroom at the airport and my luggage was still in the car. I yawned and felt a massive throb in my temples. *Urgh, jet-lag!* I cursed and to get rid of my headache, I walked to the cafeteria to get the best cure of headache in the world, a cup of tea, or in his slang, a *cuppa.* I knew it was not the kind of tea we Indians were used to cherish, but it would have to do.

I ordered the beverage and sat in a corner. Many employees were having their breakfast in the cafeteria. And in here, I drew a little less attention. I guessed the white walls of the cafeteria somehow camouflaged me due to my attire.

I sipped the tea and choked. It was worse than I had hazarded. Maybe I could find someone in the kitchen who would be willing to learn to make a good *cuppa,* I thought. After all, I personally knew the boss, I snickered quietly as I opened the book I had picked up from the reception with the title 'History of the Malani Group'. I was smiling, or maybe 'ogling' would be a better word, at his super-handsome face that was displayed on the cover of the book when someone spoke, "Hi, may I join you?"

I looked up, expectantly. I was very *very* eager to meet him but unfortunately it was not someone he would send to deliver the message to call me upstairs. My first instinct was to shoo this intruder away, but I had been specifically asked to be calm and polite to all around! So I nodded courteously and he sat down opposite me.

"You are new here," he remarked, loosening his tie. He was wearing full-sleeves blue shirt and grey trousers. His shoes were a bit unkempt and his hair was in a disarray.

"I am," I smiled a little less warmly than usual.

"Awesome," and he sneaked a look at the side table. Half a dozen boys were staring at us with bated breath and I felt he was in front of me just to prove his daring to them.

I smiled and waved at all of them, just to be polite. They all looked away immediately.

"They are kind of scared of you," the man grinned. "I am Thomas," he extended his hand and I shook it gently. "And you are?" he asked, still holding my hand in his.

"Not important," I replied casually as I freed my hand from his grasp.

"Ohkay," he whistled as he leaned in.

"Are you here for an interview?" he asked eyeing the folder I had lying next to me.

"I am," I started and he clapped his hands merrily.

"It would be so awesome if you got the job, which I am sure you will," he grinned toothily.

"I like your confidence but –" I started again.

"Oh, don't worry," he brushed his hand in the air, "your folder talks about you a lot. You will get the job like that," and he snapped his fingers. "Which department are you applying in?"

"Umm… analytics," I replied.

"Hmm… there is 'supposed' to be a new Head of Analytics joining us from this week," he spoke scathingly, "But I am sure you will get the job."

"Supposed?" I asked with raised eyebrows.

"Oh, yes, some bimbo from India who caught the boss's eye. She did some magic on him and he is, well, a sucker for beautiful girls," he laughed airily.

I resisted an urge to smack that laugh from his face. How dare he!

"You just make sure you don't go in front of the big boss, okay?" he continued with a shrill laugh.

"Why?" I asked, fisting my fingers under the table. Many boys from the nearby table noticed my gesture. They tried to gain his attention to stop him, but he was unstoppable.

"Well, a beauty like you will make him fall on the ground," and he laughed again. Was this flattery?

Feeling exceptionally irked, I looked at the book 'History of the Malani Group' and opened it to show him that I was not interested in his rubbish talk anymore but it didn't dissuade him.

"I can tell you more about the Malani Group and its owners than this pathetic piece of publicity," he barked a laugh.

"Pathetic piece of publicity?" I asked, finally giving him my full attention.

"Oh, yes, this book doesn't tell the truth regarding what goes on within the walls of these offices," he spoke with guarded expressions.

"And what do you mean by it?" I asked seriously.

Feeling he has finally won me over with his garbage words he spoke, "Oh, haven't you heard," his face was full of shock and surprise.

"Heard what?" I asked curiously.

"Oh, Mr Malani is quite the ladies' man. You should be aware, alright!" he informed seriously. "I would be fired for telling you this but he pounces on every woman who enters his office. He picks one woman per month and sleeps with her round the clock, even takes her along for pleasure on business trips. He went to India a few months ago, he took several girls there, you know, just to, you know not get bored at night."

My blood boiled at these words. I just fisted my fingers and gritted my teeth to keep quiet. I had been strictly asked to maintain a calm façade at all costs, and I seriously didn't wish to lose my demeanour for this low life!

"And you are an Indian, isn't it?" he continued misjudging my expressions and body language. "He is bunking with some Indian whore, no offence to you obviously."

"Indian whore?" I asked with raised eyebrows. My heart was pounding in my chest now, and I was this close to slapping him squarely on the face.

"Yes, some married gold digger. She left her husband to sleep with Malani, poor bastard really!" he shook his head sarcastically. "Well, I have heard that she is incredibly beautiful, and Malani does have a weakness towards Indian ethnicity given he is of the same origin, but she cannot be prettier than you are, so be very careful if you ever have to step inside Malani's chambers, okay?" he folded his hands vehemently.

"Please, leave," I whispered angrily.

"What?" he looked taken aback. "I am just warning you. I don't want you to be molested –"

"One more word and I swear," I breathed heavily and before I knew what I was doing, I was on my feet, glaring down at him.

"Hey," he too stood up defensively, "are you one of his whores too?" he grinned.

I clenched my teeth and stared at him in disbelief. I was about to hit him when my phone buzzed and I answered with a snap, "Yes."

"Who rattled you this morning?" he asked in his loving voice.

"Someone named Thomas from—," I looked at Thomas and asked, "Which department you are in?"

"Finance," Thomas replied nervously.

"Someone named Thomas from Finance," I repeated into the phone.

I saw Thomas fidget nervously.

"You are in office already?" he asked sharply. "Why didn't you tell me?"

"Weren't you busy?" I asked, still glaring at Thomas, who looked exceptionally scared now.

"I am sending someone downstairs and please, baby, don't spoil your mood so early in the morning, okay," he spoke. "Where are you anyway?"

"Came for a cuppa to your cafeteria," I informed.

"That's why Nadine is unable to find you," his laughter boomed over the phone. "She is in cafeteria," he informed someone on the other line. "Listen, sweetie," he continued as he talked to me, "Nadine will come down and fetch you upstairs. Okay?"

"Okay," I sighed as I saw Thomas eagerly waiting for me to end the call. Whom did he think I was talking to?

"See you in five," and he disconnected the call.

"Ready for your interview?" Thomas asked flirtatiously. "Let me prep you," and he made to pull my folder but I placed my hand firmly on it.

"Or I can prep you verbally, I am sure you are well-versed with whatever you are hiding in there," he winked.

I felt agitated at his actions.

"Are you always this flirtatious and persistent?" I asked, sitting back and crossing my arms.

"Not really, you have sparked a unique interest in me," he grinned again.

"Does everyone think that the new Head of Analytics is a dud bimbo who ensnared your big boss?" I asked seriously.

"Yeah, kind of," he shrugged, "someone from India, already married, you know the usual qualities of a gold-digger."

Anger flared in me as my mother's voice echoed in my head at these words. I didn't know how to react to this. I was about to turn to his friends and ask the same question but Nadine entered the cafeteria at that moment. A hushed silence fell around as the big boss's personal secretary zoomed inside.

"A very good morning, ma'am," Nadine spoke as she bowed courteously in front of me.

Thomas's jaw dropped as I stood up and greeted her with a hug. I had talked to Nadine on phone multiple times since our engagement but it was the first time I was meeting her in person. She had a long and a very strict looking face. She had finely cut hair with side-partition. And she was wearing a knee-length purple dress.

"Morning, Nadine," I forced a smile in her direction.

"Welcome to our London office, ma'am. It is such a pleasure to have you here. Mr Malani is waiting for you upstairs," she beamed at me.

Thomas stammered as he too stood up, Nadine glared at him, "Y-yo- you are Nadine."

"Mr Malani is waiting for you upstairs," she smiled at me, ignoring Thomas completely.

"Y-yo-*you*..." Thomas pointed at me.

"Gold digging, divorced, persistent, dud, bimbo, whore at your service," I pouted and jerked my head in his direction.

"What?" Nadine screeched. If there was silence before, now there was absolute stillness.

"Nothing, Nadine," I shook my head.

"Did you call her a gold --- Oh my God!" Nadine continued in the same agitated tone. "Do you have any idea who she is?"

"I — I didn't know," Thomas started again.

"Do you have any idea who she is marrying?" Nadine barked. Thomas swallowed nervously. "And you called her a whore?" she whispered the last word.

"Let's go, Nadine," I started to walk out. But she didn't. She grabbed Thomas's ID card that was hanging around his neck and pulled it out of its holder.

"I—" Thomas tried to speak but no words came out. He looked on the verge of fainting.

I took back the ID card from her hand and put in Thomas's shirt pocket.

"You won't do anything, Nadine," I ordered, "Not even tell Shaun, alright?"

Nadine stared at me in disbelief, "But, ma'am, he insulted you."

"Sometimes getting insulted is the best way to know where you are headed. And thanks to Thomas here, I know what battles I am up against," I smiled ruefully.

Yes, I was upset by his words but they did give me deep insights in the goings around here. I always knew I had to work very hard to win over the senior management, but I didn't know that I had to prove myself to every single employee of the Malani Group. "Now, let's not keep Shaun waiting, shall we. I cannot wait to meet him." And with one final wave in Thomas's direction, which he didn't return obviously, we walked away.

Chapter 2

"He should be punished, ma'am," Nadine fumed as we waited for the elevator.

"We cannot punish everyone," I replied simply. I was trying to keep a calm façade, but I was feeling epically down. Well, who wouldn't after listening to such disparaging words.

"People need to respect you," Nadine continued earnestly.

"Respect is earned, and I am sure, as they will get to know me, they will come around," I smiled, despite my feelings.

"I am in full mood to get that Thomas fired. If Mr Malani found out, he would fire him in the blink of an eye," Nadine spoke as we stepped inside the elevator.

"We cannot fire everyone who talks ill about me," I sighed, now feeling humiliated. More than Thomas's words, it was Nadine's reaction that was bothering me!

"Oh, for you, he will fire everyone, and I mean everyone," Nadine confirmed.

We reached the top floor and though the elevator doors opened, I didn't step out, gloom finally taking root in my heart.

The doors closed again and Nadine stopped the elevator by pressing the big 'STOP' button as she turned to look at me.

"Put on a big smile, ma'am," she encouraged by displaying her slightly yellowish teeth.

I huffed and asked, "Is that how everyone sees me? Indian whore? Gold digger?" I asked solemnly.

"Not the people whose opinions matter," Nadine spoke in a matter-of-fact tone, "Don't let what others think of you put you down. They all want to be where you are, so obviously they are going to act out," she shrugged.

I exhaled heavily and looked at the elevator doors, finally feeling my eyes burn.

"Should we head out?" she asked and I looked at my reflection in the elevator panel. The confidence from before had escaped my saddened pores and it looked like I had deflated slightly.

Nadine paused and added, "Mr Malani is going to shoot me for keeping you away from him," she laughed, "but know this, he loves you. I have worked with Mr Malani for years now. I was his assistant when he started working under his father, and I have seen him grow. I have seen him struggle and I have seen him fight and win. I have seen him at his lowest, and I have seen him at his peak. Until last year I had thought I have seen him in all phases of life, even his highest, but I was wrong. You are his new high! He loves you more than you can even comprehend. His life is not easy, but you make it bearable for him. You have no idea how stupid he has been, please excuse the term, but ever since you have informed him about your arrival, he has been acting like a stupid teenager who is hopelessly in love. And his stupidity has reached its peak since you have boarded the plane and it has surpassed that peak from the moment you have landed," she laughed affectionately. "He was in a board meeting and there was a fight going on about something inside. That's why I requested you to stay downstairs because his undivided attention was needed there, but realizing the time, he just dismissed everyone in the middle of the meeting, or should I say fight. There was an uproar, and while he was settling it, he sent me to the cafeteria to get you," she paused to smile, "He loves you, okay. He doesn't consider you whatever others may see you to be. So please, put on a smile your future husband deserves and go meet him with the same ecstasy with which he is waiting for you," and Nadine showed her phone to me, which displayed the caller ID name. Shaun was calling her.

I rubbed my hands on my face roughly to gain my focus and she gasped.

"What?" I asked, shocked by her gasp.

"May I?" she asked, extending her hands.

"What?" I asked, perplexed.

She grabbed my palms and stared at them.

"What?" I asked again, too shocked now.

"Wow," she whispered as she peered at my face intently. "One day, maybe when you trust me enough, you can tell me how you are so beautiful without any make-up."

Understanding her meaning, I laughed. "Oh, it's not a big deal," I dismissed her casually. "It's all about eating good and right," and with a wink and a smile, I gestured her to take me to my future husband.

♥

As the elevator doors opened, I felt I had entered a different world altogether. Fourteenth floor was like an oval dome, lined with glass all around. A small cluster of desks was in middle of the dome, which too was in the oval form.

"This is the C-suite floor and you will find all the top personnel here," Nadine informed me as she pointed around the glass wall. "We secretaries sit out here, while all executives are inside. All the glasses are covered with reflective panes, so be advised that anyone inside can see you presently," and she led me to the farthest corner which had a door with words inscribed on it:

SHAUN MALANI,
MANAGING PARTNER & CEO

My lips quivered into a smile as I stared at his name.

"Shall we, ma'am?" Nadine asked as she placed her hand on the door handle.

But I didn't move. I couldn't help but stare at his name. The name that was now my life. I raised my hand and caressed it lovingly when the door opened, startling me.

"How long do I have to wait for you to enter?" he grinned as he grabbed my already raised hand and pulled me in.

"Nadine, make sure no one, literally, no one disturbs me," Shaun laughed as he hugged me and lifted me in his arms.

Nadine bowed and closed the door behind her.

"Oh, I missed you," he smiled as he faced me and placed his lips firmly on mine. And as his lips touched me, I forgot everything. I forgot what people were talking about me, what labels they were giving and even the gossip that was following me around. All I remembered now was why I was here and what I truly desired.

Him. And only him.

"So what kept you and what made you so upset?" he asked as he pulled back.

"Nothing important, and I missed you too," I spoke, chewing my lips.

"Don't do that," he whispered, grabbing my chin and pulling my lower lip from under my teeth. "Only I can do that," and before I could answer, he had pressed his lips on mine again pushing himself firmly on me and a moan of desire for him left my lips.

I grabbed his collar and pulled him closer. Meeting my passion in hunger for him equally, he kissed me fiercely. I wrapped my hands around his neck and I felt his one hand tangle in my hair, and another hand slide inside my shirt and clutch the skin of my back. As his nails grazed my back, I felt a different sense of ecstasy rush through me.

We were entangled in a bubble of passion and desire when the door to his office flung open and someone walked inside, Nadine following hurriedly.

"I am so sorry, sir, I tried to stop her," Nadine apologized furiously.

Shocked by this sudden arrival, I pulled back but Shaun held me to him. His lips were still on me when he pulled back slightly, exhaled through his mouth, his breath glistened my face and without looking at who had entered, he spoke, "Just leave."

"This looks classy," a woman spoke from our side. "Nadine, you can go," she ordered.

Puffing loudly, Shaun punched the wall behind me, pressed his face in my shoulder for a moment to control his temper, then slowly withdrawing his hand from under my shirt, he stepped back.

"Hello, Mia," Shaun addressed grudgingly as he looked at me from top to toe, buttoned my shirt, which I didn't know was open now, and turned.

Though I was too smitten to face the intruder of our private moment, my head jerked towards the woman at the name Mia.

Mia was the female version of Shaun. She had a perfect oval face with big almond eyes, which had smoky look at present. Her hair was long and blonde, and there was an elegance with which she carried herself. She was wearing wine coloured one-shoulder dress with matching heels and bag, and she looked exceptionally beautiful.

"Hello, brother," Mia looked at me with narrowed eyes, dropped her bag in a chair, and turned to face us with arms crossed at the front, "You must be Kaya."

"Yes, she is," Shaun spoke, wrapping his hand around my waist and pulling me forward to meet his sister.

I extended my hand to shake Mia's, but she didn't oblige. She was looking at me like I was an untouchable. Well, she was royalty I would never argue against it, but I was sterling too, at least enough to be Shaun's better-half!

"I heard you cancelled a board meeting today," Mia's tone was scathing, "Despite the arguments and accusations that were being thrown at you?"

"Oh, you mean the board meeting you were supposed to attend as you too are a member of the board but missed because – ?" Shaun asked, sitting on his table and pulling me with him. He was not willing to let go off me. Maybe he was worried I would run away due to the hatred Mia was showing towards me.

"I was busy," Mia shrugged. "Are the rumours true?"

Shaun shrugged, placed his chin on my shoulder and tightened his grip around my waist, "I am just too busy to care…"

"Can't you stand on your own?" Mia demanded, who too noticed how Shaun was dragging me all around.

"Oh, she can," Shaun laughed as he planted a kiss on my neck. I looked at him scoldingly so he added, "But I've met her after four long months today, so I am not letting her go that easily."

"You can fuck her all you want, just stay within the boundaries while you have company," Mia taunted and my jaw dropped at her words.

"I didn't ask for your company, you are inflicting it on me," Shaun retorted.

"Are you forgetting all our offices have cameras?" Mia asked. "Or were you deliberately giving our security a few free porn shows," she laughed manically.

I looked at Shaun in disbelief, who shook his head to indicate there were no cameras in his office.

"Fine, I am here to tell you and your *whatever* a few things," Mia started.

"My *fiancée,*" Shaun growled.

Mia rolled her eyes and clicked her tongue in a bored way. I gripped Shaun's hand to compose myself. However, Mia was quite observant, she raised her eyebrows as my gesture didn't go unnoticed by her.

"Want to hit me?" she asked.

I just glared at her, unable to find enough words to express my hatred.

"Well, feeling's mutual, sister," she continued, "But your bodyguard or should I say your body salvager here won't let me have my way with you."

"That's enough, Mia," Shaun scolded her.

"Fine," Mia smiled pathetically. "Mom wants to meet *her,*" she pointed at me, "but she had to leave for California as *maasi* fell down the stairs and injured her hip."

"Is *maasi* okay?" Shaun asked quickly.

"I don't know, okay," Mia looked severely bored.

"But mom asked me to pass on the following instructions to you. She wanted to tell them to you herself but you didn't take her calls this morning, did you? She left you a note, alas, with me, which I read, obviously," and she pulled out a paper from her bag and waved it in Shaun's face. Shaun started to take it but Mia didn't let him. "She too should listen," she smirked and read, "First, *Kaya will not come to our home until I am back.*"

"What? Why?" Shaun demanded.

"Answer is in the second," Mia rolled her eyes, "*Kaya will not sleep in Shaun's bed at any cost before she is his legal wife…*" she paused, "Seriously, wife! Her? You couldn't have found someone brand new?"

"Like you are a Virgin Oil, are you?" Shaun barked, "She is more chaste than you are, sis… at least she doesn't go slutting around with random men in pubs."

Mia's jaw dropped for a second, then composing herself she spoke, "No, she just goes slutting around the most eligible bachelors of the world, doesn't she?"

"What? Mia—" I spoke finally.

"Important people speaking here," she waved her finger towards herself and Shaun. "And to you, it is Amelia, Ms Amelia Malani."

Shaun started to speak, "Mia, that's –"

But she read the third point from the list, "***Shaun is to not have any kind of physical relationship with Kaya in his office***... Mom knows you so well, bro..." she laughed, "Good thing I stopped by, didn't I?" and she laughed again.

"What else?" Shaun demanded in an enraged tone.

"Let's see..." and Mia read through the points, "Wedding plans, family matters, her ex-husband and yes, last one, she doesn't want to have any illegitimately conceived grandchildren, so please refrain," and giving me a vicious look, she placed the paper with a thump on his table, and left, swinging her bag on her arms.

Chapter 3

"So, that's Mia – oh sorry, I mean Ms Amelia Malani!" I spoke sarcastically, finally freeing my waist from his grasp and walking a little away from him.

"Yes, that's my sister," Shaun huffed as he picked up the paper Mia had so dramatically thumped on the table and read through it. I looked at him. He was lost deep in his mother's words while I blinked back tears. She was the second person who had called me 'gold digger and whore' in the past hour. What was happening here? Was my mother right? Was coming here the biggest mistake of my life?

Recalling, my luggage was still in the car which had driven me here from the airport, quietly, I walked out of the door. Nadine was sitting on her desk right outside his office. She looked up at me but I didn't pay heed to her expressions. I was by the elevator when he caught up with me.

"Where are you going?" he asked from a distance.

The elevator door opened and without sparing him a look, I walked in and pressed the big 'G' on the panel with my back to him.

"Hey, wait," I heard him call but the elevator doors closed and it descended from the fourteenth floor to the ground floor. The doors opened and I quickly wiped my face to get rid of the tears that were staining my cheeks and walked to the receptionist.

"Please call –" I checked the name of the driver who had dropped me to the office, "David. He is the driver who drove me here."

The receptionist was still on the phone when her eyes widened in shock. I knew pretty well who was standing behind me now but I didn't turn. He placed his hand on the counter beside me and whispered in my ears, "Where are you going?"

"Out," I replied in the same hushed tone, trying to swallow the lump in my throat. People all around us were staring now. "Please, call David, he has my luggage," I requested the receptionist, who looked at Shaun fearfully. Shaun must have nodded because the receptionist did the needful.

"Ask him to bring the car out front," Shaun ordered and wrapping his hand around my waist, he started to lead me out the main door.

"Sir, ma'am..." a voice called, "Mr Malani sir."

Shaun turned, though I didn't. I had recognized the voice.

"Please, Ms Pradhan, I am truly sorry. Please do not fire me," Thomas begged.

"What?" Shaun asked, perplexed.

"I didn't mean to call you –" Thomas cried. "If you will fire me, I will be dead. Please, I am sorry."

"Who fired you and why?" Shaun asked seriously.

"You are not fired," I whispered with my back to the men. If Mia, *his sister,* could call me a slut, what was Thomas. I turned to the receptionist and asked her to dial Nadine's number.

"This is Nadine," Nadine answered at the first ring.

"Kaya here," I sighed.

"Yes, Kaya, are you –" she started.

"You will not fire Thomas," I ordered.

"What?" Nadine was shocked.

"Yes, no firing on my account. Do you hear me?" I continued in the same tone.

"But –" Nadine spoke.

"NO FIRING," I repeated with a serious stress.

"Fine. Thomas can keep his job!" Nadine spoke.

"Good," and without another word, I gave the phone to the receptionist, who looked equally shocked.

"Thank you, Ms Pradhan. I cannot express –" Thomas started but I didn't listen to him. I saw David arrive at the front of the office, and I walked out as my own mother's words echoed in my ears.

♥

Two days ago, when I was still in India

"Wow, so now you won't even reply to me?" my mother howled with rage.

"What is it you want me to tell you, mother," I sighed as I bent to pull a dress and winced slightly. The wound in my belly often ached when I was stressed or bent suddenly. And frustrated with my mother, I was in both situations, stressed and bent down!

"Why are you moving across the world?" she asked again, paying no heed to my pained expressions. "You will have no one there, we all are here, you will be all alone."

"I won't be alone, mom, I have Shaun," I replied massaging my stomach to ease the pain.

"Is that all? You are going there just to be with him?" she spat venomously.

"And I have work, mom. Technically, I am posted in London," I tried to reason, even though I knew it was futile.

"You can work from here. You can get a transfer to India. He deliberately gave you London so that you both can be together," she barked.

"The position I hold, I cannot operate from anywhere except the headquarters of Malani Group, and that is in London," I spoke.

"Is that all?" she raised her eyebrows and crossed her arms. "Tell the truth, I raised you better," she ordered.

"Fine, mom. I am going there to be with Shaun. Happy? I love him, I miss him terribly and I cannot wait to see him," I answered honestly.

"But he doesn't miss you. He has visa and a private plane and whatnot, but he doesn't come and meet you. He doesn't care enough to come see you. But you have to run away and go there," she snapped.

"He misses me, not you," I muttered under my breath. Arsh, my brother, who was sitting in my room, witnessing all drama, snickered.

"Why doesn't he come here?" my mother continued, ignoring both me and Arsh.

"Because I am here, mom, in Nashik, in my parents' house," I exclaimed, unsure about how to reply to her accusations.

"Are you ashamed of this house?" my mom demanded and I slapped my forehead in exasperation.

"Oh, mom!" I heaved a sigh, "I am not ashamed of anything. You may be ashamed of my choices, but I am not ashamed of anything. Not of my divorce, not of loving Shaun, not of you guys, not of this house. It's just that you and Shaun don't see eye to eye, and if he came and lived here, even for a day, you both will kill each other."

"He is not welcome in this house," my mother twisted her mouth.

"He is, of course, welcome in this house," my father spoke from outside. Arsh and I snickered as we looked at each other.

"Fine, I am always outvoted," my mother barked.

"Well, you always bet on the losing horse, mom," Arsh mouthed.

"Arsh!" I scolded him.

"Wait for it…" he grumbled. And sure enough, my mother spoke after a second's pause, "Are you sure you don't want to get back with Daksh? He is such a nice man; he loves you so much. You too loved him so much. He –"

"She is not getting back with Daksh," my father dictated from the next room and I could not be more grateful to him.

"Why?" my mother shouted.

"Because somethings just do not go hand in hand in a happy marriage and domestic violence is one of them," my father finally made his appearance in my room and looked around. My room was epically messy and presence of my entire family in it didn't help the case.

"And what she did, goes hand in hand? Sleeping with another man!" my mother roared.

There was a ringing silence at these words. Instinctively I massaged my stomach at the spot where I had stabbed myself. I never told it to anyone but every time I saw the scar in the mirror, I saw Daksh's angry, disappointed face. And though the scar still hurt sometimes, it was nothing in comparison to the guilt I still housed in my heart.

"Why? You won't say anything to her now, isn't it?" my mother continued in the same tone, "It is because of this, this –" she poked my dad's chest angrily, " – that she got so out of hand. That she slept with that goon."

"MOTHER!" I shouted too.

"I am so ashamed of you," my mother started again and I closed my eyes to calm my tears. "You have no idea what people say about you."

"What do they say? Slut? Whore? Gold digger?" I barked.

Another ringing silence in the room.

"Fine example you are setting for your younger brother!" my mother continued after a pause. "Showing him it is alright to cheat on your partner and sleep around."

I was about to retort when Arsh spoke angrily, "I am not a child, and she is not sleeping around. She loves Shaun and is marrying him. And being with someone you love is not wrong."

"I would bury you alive if you slept with someone before marriage," my mother raged. "See," she snarled at me, "what you are doing here. Setting wrong standards."

"I am almost thirty," I spoke through gritted teeth.

"Too old to listen to your mother?" she spat.

"That's why I wanted to live in Mumbai," I muttered angrily.

"Yes, in that brothel he bought for you," my mother's word rang in my ears.

"Enough!" I shouted so loudly that everyone jumped. "Enough is enough, mom. I never asked to come down here, and if you are going to insult and humiliate me every second of my life, I am –"

"What?" she demanded.

"It really is enough," my father spoke, who was just as shocked by mother's attitude.

Arsh started picking up things and started helping me pack. Controlling my tears, I too continued to pack.

"Need a hand in packing, princess?" my father asked seriously.

"Don't need a hand in packing," I sniffed.

"Call Shaun, I want to talk to him," my mother spoke.

"I am so not calling him," I rolled my tear-filled eyes at my mother.

"Why? Now he has issues in talking to me as well," she demanded.

"He likes to talk to you just as much you like talking to him..." I stated the obvious, thinking how he would come down tonight if I called him while I was tear-stricken. My pain may not bother my mother, but it did bother the man who loved me.

My mother stared at me with furious expressions then turned, "Arsh, you call him. I know he calls you often," my mother ordered and I stared at Arsh in shock.

"Oh yeah, he calls me every other day to chat, you know!" Arsh shrugged. When I just stared at him with baffled expressions, he added,"You know, to talk about you, how are you being treated and for general catch up."

My heart suddenly was full of warmth at these words. Shaun, despite being so busy, called my brother to talk about me!

"That reminds me, dad," and Arsh addressed our father, "Shaun asked me something yesterday."

Dad and I exchanged a look at this. "He wants me to apply to Harvard University."

Both me and my dad stood rooted to the ground at this.

"On full scholarship," he added and my jaw dropped. "He said I could get in on merit and he will anyway put in a word. But he said it would be good for me and will give me a boost like none other."

"What did you say?" my father asked seriously.

"And why didn't you tell me?" I scolded.

"He called me late last night, he said it just struck him because of something else, so he called me instantly as he knew he would forget later," Arsh informed.

"What did you say then?" my father asked.

"I said I will think about it," Arsh shrugged.

"What's there to think about?" my mother said and I thought that maybe for the first time she was appreciating Shaun for something, but her next words drowned that feeling, "Just say NO!"

All of us stared at her with incredulous expression.

"What do you want to do?" my father asked, ignoring my mother.

"I don't know, what do you guys suggest?" Arsh asked. "I have to start afresh there though!"

"You are already in Second year," my mother started. "Why would you waste two years of your life?"

"Harvard is not a waste of life," I rolled my eyes at her.

"You would have to uproot your life and move there," my mother started.

"She is doing it," my brother pointed at me.

"That's amazing, simply amazing! That goon is not just stealing my daughter, he is also taking my son from me," my mother spat.

"This is the last time you are calling him a goon, I so mean it, mom," I threatened.

"What? He is a *gunda! Gunda,* I tell you. Threatening me, Daksh, that poor doctor. Dictating your life, bossing everyone around. You really want to be in his debt, Arsh? You don't know how we may have to repay for his 'recommendation'!"

I closed my eyes and exhaled heavily to compose myself. If she weren't my mother, I swear I would have killed her!

"I think now you know why he doesn't come here," I snapped.

"We are not taking any favours from him," my mother thundered.

"He is not doing any favour," now it was Arsh who spoke. "He cares for me just as much..." he paused uncomfortably, "well, just as much Daksh did, and only better. At least Shaun's care is bringing something good in my life, all Daksh did was talk about stupid games. And he cares for and loves my sister more than anything. I think I am going to take him up on the offer."

"Favours," my mother spat.

"Doing things for family is not a favour, mom," I sighed.

"He is not our family," my mother continued in the same tone.

"He is mine," I started.

"I hope you will not repay this and other favours in ways we don't approve of," my mother muttered.

"That's enough," my father interjected. "I think she needs some space to pack and have some peace."

"I am hindering her peace?" my mother challenged.

"Yes, at present you are," my father accused.

"I –" my mother started but Arsh added, "Take your fight to your room, guys! I just have tonight to spend quality time with my sister."

♥

Present Day - London

I sat in the car from one side, while David rushed to open the door for Shaun, who sat beside me.

"Where to, sir? Ma'am?" David asked.

"Airport, please," I answered and Shaun looked utterly shocked.

"Umm, no!" Shaun corrected. "Take us to the Airia," he ordered.

David nodded and started to drive. Unsure of what 'Airia' was, I just sat in silence beside him, tears dropping occasionally from my eyes. Shaun, feeling defeated, gave me his handkerchief to wipe my face but I ignored him.

"What did that guy say to you?" Shaun demanded. I didn't reply to him again.

He looked furious at my silence and dialled Nadine to demand the same thing. However, Nadine didn't stay quiet and told him everything. Shaun was beside himself with rage.

"Oh, he is so fired," Shaun barked. "How dare he!"

I snatched his phone from his hand and spoke, "I told you and I am repeating it, HE IS NOT FIRED!" and I disconnected the call.

Shaun was about to retort but the car stopped, and the driver opened the door for Shaun, while another valet opened the door for me.

'Airia' was nothing but the name of a house. Well, it was not a house, it was a mansion.

"I am not supposed to be here," I spoke through gritted teeth.

"This is not my 'home' home," Shaun replied, grabbing my waist and leading me in, "It is another house. I have many properties in London!"

I let him lead me inside as I knew there was no use fighting at this moment. I would leave a little later.

"Ask Sarina and staff to arrange the luggage in wardrobe of my room later," Shaun ordered as he led me upstairs. If I was not as upset as I was feeling at the moment, I would have appreciated the enormous house. It was huge... way bigger than any normal house I had ever seen. The living room, or whatever it was called here in London, was four times the size of my apartment in India.

As we entered his room, he closed the door behind us and made me turn to face him.

"What did you mean by 'airport'? And we will get back to the airport business, why didn't you say anything about what that pervert said to you?" he glared at me.

"I now know it was a mistake coming here," I replied simply as I walked away from him and went inside the bathroom. He didn't wait for me outside but barged inside before I could lock it.

"What do you mean by a mistake?" he demanded.

"I need to use the washroom," I informed.

"Feel free to do so, I am not leaving until you answer me," he crossed his arms and stared at me, fuming.

I looked at him in disbelief, then turned to wash my face.

"Please talk to me," he groaned as he hugged me from behind and pressed his forehead on my neck. "Just don't talk about leaving, please. I just got you here."

"I don't belong here," I sighed, fresh tears falling from my eyes.

"You belong with me, and I live here," he added.

I pushed him and walked out. He followed me like a lost puppy.

"I should have assigned your Detail the moment you landed. I was planning to pick you up but that stupid meeting took precedence. If you had security around you, that pervert would not have dared utter those words to you," he fisted his fingers angrily. "He will be punished," he added.

"Why?" I demanded.

"What why? How dare he?" he started.

"Just the way your sister dared!" I snapped. "They both said exactly the same thing. The only additional things Thomas said were about you, are you punishing him because he bad-mouthed you?" I demanded.

"What? NO!" he looked thunder-struck.

"They both called me 'gold digger'. They both called me 'whore'. In comparison to what your sister said, Thomas's words were politer," I barked.

"He called you a whore?" Shaun asked, wide-eyed.

"And your sister called me one to your face," I snapped.

"She didn't call you a 'whore'," Shaun looked at me with disbelief, "She wouldn't dare!"

"Not in exact words but –" I started.

"No words at all, Kaya," Shaun shook his head. "Mia is difficult. She is a brat. She is worse than she lets out, believe me," he explained and now I was shocked. *Worse than she lets out?!*

"She can and will make our lives immensely difficult if she decided on it, so I didn't —" he tried to explain.

"You didn't defend me," I interrupted.

"All I did was defend you," Shaun looked too shocked to express. "Please recall the conversation, even though it was not pleasant. I asked her to go away. She read out mom's words, I called her 'Virgin Oil' or something, then she left after leaving mom's instructions behind."

"Well?" Shaun demanded as I didn't reply.

"You didn't defend hard enough," I retorted.

"I knew it would have spurred Mia on," he explained heavily, "But I am sorry. I truly am for hurting you."

I looked away so he grabbed my face in his hands and made me look in his beautiful gold flecked black eyes, "I am really, truly, deeply sorry. I love you and there is nothing more important to me in this whole damn world."

Another tear trickled down my cheek. He kissed it away and licked his lips, "Salty," he grinned.

When I didn't smile back, he begged, "Please, don't make me chase you all the way back to India, please… it is good we have four elevators, else I would have had to run down fourteen flights of stairs for you today. And you made the whole office shake as I never go to the ground floor ever. My presence scares the shit out of people there. I am sorry," he repeated.

Freeing myself from his grasp, I sat on the bed. He sat in front of me on his knees and placed his head on my thighs. "Promise to not run away to India?"

I didn't know what to do but I wanted him more than anything in the whole world. I loved him enough to fight all slangs and accusations people may throw at me.

"Please?" he begged again.

"Only on one condition," I croaked.

"Anything," he looked up.

"You will let me go pee whenever I want to in peace…" I smiled finally.

"What alone? Always?" he asked, laughing and sitting back on the floor.

"Yes," I stood up and walked to the bathroom. "Always," and I closed the bathroom door on his face, which was alight with happiness now.

Chapter 4

That evening Shaun left to put out the fire that had started in the board meeting that morning. He didn't want to, but with the number of calls he was getting, non-stop from all around the world, he decided to leave.

However, before leaving, he introduced me to the staff of Airia. There were way too many people catering to house that had no regular dwellers, well, until now.

Sarina was my hand-maiden, I didn't know I was to get one, or it was actually a norm to have one in a household! And she had a handful of girls working underneath her to ensure I am taken care of properly.

"How high maintenance do you think I am?" I had asked Shaun that afternoon when I had seen so many girls standing in front of me. "And I think I can do my own stuff, I am used to it," I muttered.

"But you don't have to now, do you," Shaun had laughed, kissed me lightly and then left.

Sarina introduced me to everyone and told me what her job was. She was there to ensure all my needs were fulfilled without uttering a word. I wondered what kind of work she was supposed to do, but understood that very evening when I arrived in my room and found my night clothes laid for me on the bed.

I was stunned by this.

"Is it not what you would like to wear tonight?" one of the girls asked. She looked scared.

"It is fine," I replied, feeling weird at this development. "You will also see to what I wear each day to office?" I asked, perplexed.

"We will take care of everything. All you need to do is indicate if you want something else and we will do it," she smiled.

I nodded and she left. As I was severely jet-legged, I changed into my night clothes and climbed into the bed. And I was asleep even before I had any dinner.

♥

The next morning Shaun and I had breakfast together and went to the office.

"This is your office," Shaun beamed with happiness as he showed me a door that was two offices down his and read 'Kaya Malani – Chief Marketing Officer'

My jaw dropped at the words that were displayed at the door – both my name 'Kaya Malani' and the designation.

I decided to confront about the designation first. "Wasn't I supposed to be 'Analytics Head'?" I demanded.

"Well," he grinned. "I know I said we will take it slow, but then I thought, what the heck! This is my company, my wife... so, I promoted you," he shrugged carelessly and my jaw dropped.

Laughing still, he closed my mouth with his finger.

"And what about the name here?" I asked with raised eyebrows.

"I know you are not officially mine, well you are, but you know legally," he smirked as he held me in his arms in the middle of the floor, "But I don't want to read 'Kaya Pradhan' here. I like the sound of this –" and he pointed at the name again.

"But I *am* Kaya Pradhan," I whispered as all the secretaries on the floor were giving us sly glances. "Not unless we are married officially."

"Well, that's one conundrum I think we can resolve if you wish to, much sooner than later," he grinned as he opened the door for me and I entered. The office was exact replica of Shaun's office. The furniture and décor were same. The only difference was, the laptop placed on the big table was mine and not his!

"Cameras are all around the floor and office," he pointed at the wall, "It is visuals only camera so your calls are not overheard," he continued, "This is your seat," he pointed at the big boss's chair, "And now it is up to you how bright you shine."

I nodded, feeling awkward.

"Why don't you get settled here and then maybe, in the evening, we can christen this office?" he whispered and laughed.

"What about cameras?" I asked, shocked.

"They can be disabled at just one call," he laughed and bent down to kiss me.

"Umm..." he moaned as he pulled back, "...maybe we should wrap things up sooner!"

"Maybe," I replied, a little out of breath too.

"Should I ask for camera disablement now?" he whispered in my ears.

"What?" I asked, coming back to my senses. "NO!" I pushed him back.

"You really need to adjust your face then," he laughed, kissed me lightly on my cheek and pressed a button on the intercom on my desk.

"Kaya Malani's office," a voice spoke and I felt goosebump erupt on my body at the words.

Shaun muted the intercom and beamed at me, "I like the sound of it, Kaya Malani," then unmuting the intercom, he ordered, "Come in."

"Sit," he pointed at the boss's chair with a smile, and I moved to it slowly, though I didn't sit down. I felt awkward.

"Good morning, sir, ma'am," a girl knocked and entered. She was a lean girl, had her hair tied in a neat bun and was wearing white shirt and blue skirt.

"She is Alia, she is your personal secretary," Shaun informed me.

Well, if he got me a personal hand-maiden, a secretary was an obvious addition.

"Hello, ma'am, it is such a pleasure to meet you," Alia walked ahead and shook my hand.

"You can go," Shaun ordered and Alia retreated.

The moment she was gone, he pushed me in the chair, kissed me on my forehead and spoke, "I am leaving for Oxford for a meeting now. I will see you for dinner, okay?"

I nodded, and he moved out. I walked with him and watched him enter his office. As I stared after him, I felt maybe I will never get used to him....

I saw Alia sitting next to Nadine, who smiled at me.

"So this is your desk," I spoke to Alia. There were a few other people sitting around the desks who were trying very hard to ignore me, but were failing!

Nadine's intercom buzzed but she didn't answer. She just got up and went to Shaun's office.

"This is my desk, Mrs Malani," Alia smiled at me, she looked very scared and uncomfortable.

"Umm... please call me Ms Kaya for now," I spoke, "Answer phone as 'Ms Kaya's office'. Drop Malani until we are officially married, okay?" And as if on cue, Shaun stepped out and pouted at these words.

"Are you sure you don't want to share names just yet?" he asked as he came up to me.

"Very sure," I smiled.

"Do as she asks. Just keep her happy," Shaun spoke to everyone around, who all smiled awkwardly.

"See you later then," he whispered in my ears, kissed me on my cheek and walked away.

I stared at his back as he stood beside Nadine, who was waiting for the elevator. The elevator dinged, and he entered. I sighed softly, but as if he heard me sigh, he stepped back, waved at me with a smile and disappeared.

I don't know why but this small gesture made my heart swell with love for him.

"Anything else, ma'am?" Alia asked gingerly.

Her question brought me back to reality.

"Yes," I exhaled, "please send me my schedule so I know what is happening and where, okay?" I commented.

"Right away, ma'am," she nodded and thus began my work in an official capacity.

♥

The week passed in a haze. Despite our plans to get free early and spend time together, well, we couldn't.

Shaun, technically, followed through his mother's orders and didn't cosy up with me. But it was not because he was the most obedient son, it was because we simply didn't get a chance. With us spending entire day working in office, and evenings spent entertaining his friends who kept on visiting us, Shaun could hardly find time to steal a kiss or two, let alone a full sleepover.

"I didn't know Shaun had so many friends," I smiled as I sat opposite another pair of couples – Philip and Andy, Cory and Sienna. The room rang with laughter while Shaun and I exchanged a pitiful glance at each other. How we wished his friends would leave us alone but we didn't know how to say it without sounding rude. Without fail, each evening, someone or other rang our doorbell and we were forced to put on our best smiles and entertain.

"Oh, you haven't met half of his friends yet," Philip roared as he chugged more beer. "He was, for obvious reasons, the most popular kid in school and college. He was friends not just with his classmates, but also with his juniors and seniors."

"What obvious reasons," I asked politely.

"Umm ... haven't you met the guy who has his arms around you?" Philip laughed.

"Easy on the beer, darling," Philip's girlfriend, Andy, stopped him from emptying yet another can.

"Well, it's party night tonight," Philip laughed, "I am gonna drink the whole fucking London today."

I blinked back my surprise at these words as I yawned.

"You are tired?" Shaun asked, rubbing my back.

"It is 2 in the morning," I whispered as I leaned back in his arms. "I have a meeting at 7 with India."

"Why so early?" Shaun asked, placing his chin on my shoulder.

"Because I also have Maria from New Zealand on the call to discuss a new marketing dashboard we are building," I yawned again.

"I would love to know what this new dashboard will do," he smiled in my ears as he planted a few kisses down my neck. "Good thing, tomorrow is Friday... then finally we will have the weekend to ourselves."

"Should we leave the room," Philip snickered.

"Nah, I think Kaya will leave the room now. She is too tired and has an early meeting tomorrow," Shaun explained.

"How are you doing it?" Cory asked. He was the quiet one and talked only work. "I mean, how are you managing so many things at one go. Him I understand, he was groomed to juggle between stuff, you on the other hand, no offence please," he added quickly, "but I see you are managing more than he does!"

"Hey!" Shaun retorted with a laugh, "But you are right. She is my super-hero," and he squeezed me in his arms.

I laughed with him for his love.

"Seriously," Cory insisted, "how are you doing it?"

"I don't know," I shrugged as I finally got up to go to sleep. "I just work hard I guess."

"What motivates you?" Cory's wife, Sienna, asked.

"One thought that I don't want the world to label me as a 'Gold digger – slut' for making him fall in love with me. I want to prove to everyone that I am worthy of his love, and what other way to prove than working hard and adding value to the empire he is striving so hard to raise. I just want to show to the world that I am not just a pretty face, he fell in love with me for my brains too."

My words were met with ringing, though full of admiration, silence.

I bade everyone goodnight, ruffled Shaun's hair lovingly and walked back to our room. I could hear soft sounds of Shaun and his friends from downstairs, but I didn't care. I meant every single word of what I said. I wanted to prove to the world, especially Mia, that I was worth more than *her* to this empire. That I too was 'important'.

And with that one vengeful thought, I slumped on the bed and fell asleep.

Chapter 5

Weekend arrived finally and we had promised each other to sleep in late, stay in the bed the whole day and not open our laptops or even our door for any visitors at any cost, well not until something literally burnt down.

However, when I opened my eyes at around 9 in the morning, I didn't wake up to his beautiful face but to a note resting on his pillow.

Sorry, love, something literally burnt down so had to leave. Will be back when I can.

Miss you already, Shaun.

Feeling stung and aching all over for him, I called him. No answer! Feeling grumpy, I tossed and turned in the bed, and finally drifted off to sleep. Woke up at around 2, called him again. Again, no answer. Had a shower, lunch in solitude, watched TV shows I used to love before I met him, then dozed off to sleep. Woke up at 10, called him again. And yet! No answer. What was happening. Had my dinner. And watched some more TV. As I was majorly sleep deprived in the past week, all thanks to his friends over, I was about to sleep again when I called him around midnight.

A giggly girl answered the call.

"Hell-hihihihi-no stop-shush-hello…"

"Who is it?" I demanded.

"Oh, it is your Kaya," the girl giggled on the other side.

"Shaun, I mean Mr Malani cannot come to the phone right now, he is tied up a bit," the girl tittered again, "He said he will see you next week sometime and you should do whatever to please you – hold on, what?"

I was stunned as I distinctly heard a male voice at a distance but due to distance, I couldn't understand it.

"He wants you to go on a trip or something. Just enjoy yourself because he going to enjoy a lot tonight. He says you have earned it. Bye!"

And the line went dead, and so did my heart.

I stared at the screen of my phone for a few minutes. Who was the giggly girl? Was it really Shaun? Was it some kind of practical joke? Was he cheating on me? Post those hot, passionate twenty-fours we had spent months ago in the cottage back in India, we had not been intimate. Yes, we were sleeping in the same bed but were unable to have sex. But did it mean he was sleeping with other girls?

What did she mean by 'your Kaya', trip or something...

Hyperventilating, I looked around. Whom should I call to ask if this was some kind of joke or what? I had no friends here. My first thought was of calling Simi, my best friend in India, but how could I? It must be around 5:30 AM in India, she would kill me in her sleep if I woke her up in the wee hours. Panicking, I called the next best person. She answered on the third ring.

"Kaya, is everything alright?" Nadine answered, worried.

"Where is Shaun?" I demanded.

"With you, I presume," Nadine sounded shocked.

"If he were here, why would I call you?" I hissed.

"Sir asked me yesterday to not call either of you because he was taking the entire weekend off with you, apparently!" Nadine sounded genuinely concerned. "Should I call him?"

"No, I already did," I choked.

"And?" Nadine asked seriously.

"And nothing... we all reap what we sow," I sighed. "Have a goodnight, Nadine. I am sorry to have bothered you."

"But—" she started but I disconnected and switched off my phone.

Feeling hopelessly devastated, I slumped back in the bed and closed my eyes, though I knew sleep would not come to me easily now.

After rolling in bed for four hours in which I imagined Shaun rolling with at least forty different naked girls, I decided to take a break. If I could not even get loyalty in the name of his love then I didn't want it.

I will return to India, but not before I enjoyed my trip here, I thought scathingly. He had promised to take me around UK next month, bloody hell... I can't believe it! If he won't then it doesn't mean I cannot on my own.

I packed up a bag with things for a couple of days, used the landline to call for a self-drive cab service two streets down the Airia, and escaped the eyes of security at around 4:30 in the morning.

"First stop, Stonehenge," I spoke to myself as I added my destination in the GPS of my phone, finally turning it on after hours, and navigated through the route displayed there. It was hardly a three-hour drive.

Feeling the hurt of betrayal stabbing my heart, I started to drive. If I was not so upset, I would have enjoyed the route once I was out of London, but I couldn't. I drove slowly, real slowly because time and again my eyes were getting fogged by treacherous tears.

I was at the Stonehenge when my phone rang. It was Shaun. I disconnected it.

It rang again, and again, and again and yet again.

Feeling agitated, I finally answered. "What?" I demanded.

"What *what*?" he shouted. "Where the fuck are you?"

"On a trip, where else!" I scowled.

"WHAT? What trip? If you are back in India, I swear I will kill you," he barked.

"I am not in India, yet!" I replied sourly.

"Why was your phone off?" he demanded.

"Because I turned it off! And it is on for hours now, but well, why would you care!" I replied. "What do you want now?"

"What? Where are you?" he asked again.

"As if you care," I growled.

"What are you saying? I left you a note, didn't I?" he asked, confused.

"Oh, I got your notes… both written and voice," I hissed.

"What voice? Where are you?" he asked again.

"Stonehenge," I replied without any interest as I sat on the green grass and stared at the big stone pillars in front of me. As it was still too early, it was hardly crowded and I could enjoy the view.

"What are you doing at Stonehenge," he asked, unable to understand.

"Shaun, why don't you do one thing?" I spoke with a tinge of anger.

"What?"

"Go fuck yourself and then go to hell," and feeling epically agitated, I disconnected the call and turned the phone off again.

I didn't know what Shaun was playing at but cursing him like this felt oddly satisfying. I lay back in the grass and was only starting to feel the cold breeze that was rippling through my loose shirt when I heard the sound of a chopper.

I sat up and looked around, and there it was. A small helicopter with big M of Malani Group painted on the side. And there he was, jumping out of it, with his heavily armed guards walking beside him.

Feeling disgruntled and upset, I slumped back in the grass.

"Are you crazy?" he asked standing right on my head. I opened my eyes and saw him upside down. He was tired and angry. No, he looked livid with rage. Ignoring him, I stood up and walked up to the stone circle that was nature's miracle.

"I am talking to you," he spoke to me. But I ignored him again.

I was at the biggest stone when he grabbed my hand and pushed me against the stone. His eyes were red and he was angry beyond comprehension.

"Is this all a fucking joke to you?" he demanded, literally shouting. "You disappeared from the house, without any security, if I may add. Your phone was off, any idea how many disastrous scenarios ran through my head."

His bodyguards stepped back and turned their backs to us, forming a semi-circle. The small crowd that was already there was retreating slowly as they sensed danger.

Feeling angry myself, I pushed him hard on the chest and slapped him squarely on the face. He was so taken aback that he moved backward. His security turned to face us but he raised his hand to dismiss them.

"This is for cheating on me," I hissed as I started to walk away, but he grabbed my wrist and pushed me back to the stone. He pushed me so hard that my head hit the stone with a loud thud.

Ah! I cried as a searing pain spread through my skull and everything shifted. I pressed my head with the free hand, and though his expressions softened a bit seeing me wince in pain, he didn't leave my other hand.

"Explain," he spoke through gritted teeth.

"I don't need to explain a thing to you," the rage was making my emotions run haywire but I tried to stay focussed.

His grip tightened on my wrist as he spoke through gritted teeth again, "You hit me, explain."

"Fine… but you explain first," I demanded, pain searing all over my skull, making my eyes water.

He just glared at me.

"How was she?" I asked, rage rising in my chest again as the picture of Shaun sleeping with other naked women flashed in front of my eyes.

"She is okay," he replied, confusion replacing anger slightly.

"Wow, you have some nerve," I hissed as I tried to get free from his grip but he didn't let me go. "Let me go," I demanded but he just continued to stare at me.

"How many times?" I asked, feeling slightly diminished.

"Must be fourth," he replied.

"Four," I repeated, now feeling horribly down.

"No, five," he corrected.

And with my hand still in his, I slumped down the stone and fell on my knees, totally defeated and head pounding mercilessly.

"WHY?" I asked, crying now. But these tears were not of pity or sadness, they were of betrayal and humiliation.

"What why? You know why," he let go of my hand and took a step back.

"Yes, I know why," I whispered.

"Then why are you asking?" he demanded.

I pressed my head on the cold ground to gain some focus.

"Fine," I sighed as I spoke to the ground. "You can go do whatever with that slut, but I won't be a part of any of it."

I looked up and found him sitting in front of me.

"I called her a slut the other day but you won't call my sister a slut, okay?" he ordered.

"Oh, I will – what?" I asked, confused. "Your sister? Mia?"

"Yes, I won't allow either of you to insult each other, especially, to my face," he nodded.

"You were with Mia last night?" I asked, alarmed.

"Of course," he shrugged.

"That's… that's incest," I spat on the floor.

"In-what?" he looked so shocked that it seemed I had slapped him once more. "What did you just say?" his expressions changed horribly as he registered the word.

I looked at him quizzically. Of course, my own word was wrong.

"Did you mean?" he started.

"No-no-no… there is something wrong here," I added quickly, trying to focus hard. The pain in my head was unbearable now.

"Where were you yesterday?" I asked as calmly as possible this time.

"In Spain, trying to rescue Mia from a drunk tank," he spoke through gritted teeth. "Saving her, *not committing* incest!"

I opened my mouth to speak but closed it again, too stunned to reply.

"Didn't you see the news yesterday?" he asked, still fuming.

"No, I didn't," I replied, feeling stupid.

Scowling, he pulled up news articles from yesterday and this morning showing Mia in her bikini, fully drunk and creating scenes.

"Right! Actual fire…" I whispered, trying to focus on his phone.

"What did you think? I was sleeping with my sister?" he fisted his fingers as if trying to resist hitting me.

"You didn't pick up your call whole day yesterday," I slurred.

"You never called me. And if I didn't pick up your call, that's where your mind went? Incest?" he hissed.

"It didn't and I did call you so many times, and when at midnight that girl took the call," I continued.

"What girl?" he demanded.

"How do I know!" I exclaimed as another vision of semi-naked girls wrapped around him flashed in front of my eyes.

"The first call I received from London yesterday was from a very panicked Nadine asking my whereabouts and that you were in some kind of trouble. I called you but your phone was off. I tried for hours, then I dozed off, I came back to London and called you again, and you asked me to go to hell after fucking myself," he shouted.

I raised my phone. "I called you so many times... your phone was answered by another woman around midnight, laughing, giggling, *enjoying* with you!"

"Give me that," he snatched my phone and checked the details.

"It is not my number," he snapped and showed it to me but my vision now was too blurry to read anything. "I have two numbers, personal and business, and this number against my name on your speed dial is not mine!"

"What?" I was shocked to my core.

Grumbling still, he dialled the number and it rang, but it was not his phone that was buzzing. His phone in his other hand was quiet.

"You don't trust me," he whispered, feeling crestfallen.

"Oh, I do!" I replied feeling a heavy weight lift from my chest.

"You accused me of *incest,*" he whispered again.

"That was way too wrong, I am incredibly sorry for it," I apologized as I held my head to get some focus. "It came out accidently."

"You think I would do that with my little sister? My baby sister?" he asked in disbelief.

"Oh, no... please, I am sorry," I begged. "Out of all the scenarios that ran through my head last night, none of them was this... but the way you were answering me, it just got out of hand."

"What? You asked me how was she? I replied she was okay now! How many times I had rescued her, well, this was the fifth time I had rescued her from Madrid's drunk tank. What did I… ohhh…" he paused as an expression of comprehension dawned on his face. "You were asking, how sex with the girl was who answered my phone?"

I nodded hopelessly.

"See, I could not have guessed it because the only girl I ever wanted to have sex with was thousands of miles away from me," he replied.

"Wanted?" I asked, noticing the past tense.

"Yes, before she accused me of incest. I mean trust and all is on one side, how could you think so low of me," he barked, standing up. I too wanted to follow his action but the woozy feeling in my head didn't let me. He looked down at me for a second, then started to walk away.

"Shaun," I called, trying to get up, but just fell on my all fours. "Shaun, wait," I stood up with great difficulty and looked ahead. He was far away, almost by his chopper.

Shooting, stabbing pain was surfacing all over my head and a hot, burning sensation was following it. I took a step forward but felt the Earth shake underneath. And before I knew it, I felt myself tumbling down to the floor.

Chapter 6

When I woke up next, I was in our bed but alone. My head felt exceptionally heavy and I felt way too tired. As I touched my face, I realized a very big and tight bandage was wrapped around my forehead.

I looked at the clock on the wall, it said 2, but it could not be night time, the light straining from the curtains said it was mid-day.

"Oh, you are awake," someone spoke from the door. I looked around and saw Sarina, the maid of the house, standing there. "Good… good… finally." And she left.

She came back after another thirty minutes, in which I just lay there stupidly all alone.

"The doctor is here to see you, miss," Sarina informed and a man entered the room.

"Ms Pradhan," the doctor spoke as he sat on my bedside and examined me. "How are you feeling?"

"Fine… where is Shaun?" I asked Sarina.

"Malani sir must be in the office," Sarina informed.

"Home office?" I asked hopefully, trying to get up.

"No, office – office… he left very early today," she added.

"Today? On a Sunday? This morning we were at Stonehenge." I was shocked.

"No, dear," the doctor intervened as he flashed torchlight in my eyes, irritating me to my core. "You were at Stonehenge day before yesterday, where you had that accident."

"What?" I blanched. Did I miss two days of my life?

"Yes, and if you will stay still, I would like to examine your injuries," and he started touching my head all over. I winced as his fingers moved to the spot where I had hit my head on the rock.

"Well, you are very lucky, you only had mild swelling and it didn't do any lasting damage to your brain," the doctor sighed. "Your CT and MRI are clear, so, all you need is good rest and sleep."

"CT, MRI?" I asked, shocked.

"We did a thorough examination yesterday," he informed, as he took out a pill box and started separating multiple tablets in it. Once done, he handed the pill box to Sarina and instructed her about how to feed them to me.

"I can take my own pills," I retorted.

"But now you don't have to, do you?" Sarina smiled kindly. "We will take care of you. You just get well soon."

"One of the medicines at night has some sedative effect, so make sure you take it when you are in bed. No bathroom, changing clothes or anything after taking your medicine, do you understand me?" the doctor ordered strictly.

"Why a sedative?" I asked quizzically.

"Because it is how the medicine is," he smiled.

"Can't you give me some other?" I insisted, not willing to take a medicine that may force me to sleep and miss Shaun in the evening.

"It is not an optional medicine and I think mild sedation is good for you," he pressed his lips at this.

"Why?" I demanded.

"Because I know you people all too well… you need sleep but your thirst for wealth and booze and your 'activities' don't allow room for sleep," he mocked.

"I am not like them," I retorted.

"So I have heard, but still, you need sleep and the medicine is not an option," he sighed. "Also, no drinking after 7 –"

"I don't drink or smoke or indulge in any kind of drugs," I intervened.

"Yes, I have heard. Your future husband told me this quite proudly yesterday," he smiled. "Also, no phone or laptop for a week at least. We will see your progress then will decide further."

"But I cannot not work!" I exclaimed. "I will be bored to death. Plus, I have so much work..."

"Please take it up with your future husband, dear, he wants you to get better as quickly as possible," the doctor sighed. "I will be back for a check-up in two-days," and with one strict nod, he left.

Sarina came with a tray laden with food and waited while I ate. I was famished so I didn't need her supervision, but still, she didn't budge.

"How was Shaun today?" I asked her.

"Worried," she smiled, "he cares for you..."

I nodded, took the pills she was thrusting under my nose and lay down.

Once alone, I called up Shaun; he didn't answer.

I called again. No answer again.

I texted him. No answer again.

I called Nadine. She answered on the second ring.

"How are you feeling now?" Was her first question.

"Okay," I replied. "Would feel better if he would pick up my phone too. Is he in some meeting?"

"One second," she spoke and I heard her shuffle.

"He says, he is busy!" Nadine replied after a few seconds. "You should rest, he will call you," she added for my benefit.

"Fine," and I disconnected.

I stayed in bed all day, watched or should I say listened to TV shows as watching continuously made my head hurt, and by 9 PM I was in deep sleep, all thanks to the night pills.

Day 2 – Wednesday – When I woke up the next day, my bed was again empty.

"Good morning," Sarina came in with a wide smile.

"Shaun?" I asked.

"Left around an hour ago," she informed.

I slouched out of the bed, went to the bathroom, and when I came back found her standing with my breakfast in her hands.

And the previous day's routine began.

Day 3 – Thursday –

"Good morning," Sarina chimed. I hated her now!

"Shaun?" I grunted.

"Left two minutes ago," she informed.

I rushed to the window and saw his car speed away. Tears filled my eyes as I realized he was avoiding me. But for how long could he do that? We live in the same house after all.

When the doctor arrived to check on me and change the bandage on my head, I asked him if I could travel a bit. He was not willing but took pity on me. So after having my lunch I left for the office.

"What are you doing out of bed?" Nadine asked, pulling a chair for me. The effort of coming down to the office had drained me.

"I want to see him," I whispered.

"He is in a board meeting," Nadine pointed at the conference room. "It is going to last a while!"

"I will wait for the whole day if needed," I sighed and placed my head on her desk.

"You can lie down on the sofa in his office," Nadine suggested. I was still contemplating when the door of the conference room opened and I saw him standing there, talking to people. His eyes fell on me and he stiffened. Mia stepped out and walked towards us.

"Heard you took a fall," she grinned. "Is that your tactic always, hospital and pity!"

I didn't reply to her words. She was the reason why Shaun and I were in this mess, and I didn't want to do anything to make him hate me more.

Mia tapped her perfectly manicured nails on Nadine's desk and left with a gloating smile.

Then Shaun stepped out of the conference room with two people, and without sparing me a glance, he spoke to Nadine, "I don't want to be disturbed," and walked inside with them.

I waited for the crowd of the board members to dissipate, then left for the house too. I would not inflict my company on him.

Day 4 – Friday – I stayed home and sent a 'I am sorry' bouquet to his office while I waited hopelessly. By dinner time an idea struck, I took a note pad, created at least two hundred slips writing 'I am sorry' on each, and placed them in every single pocket of his coat, shirt, and trouser. No matter which one he wore tomorrow, he will find my note. I was still doing it when Sarina force-fed me my tablets, and I had placed the last slip in his beige coat when I fell on the floor, fast asleep.

Day 5 – Saturday – I woke up in my bed, alone, again. It was weekend and yet he was not here. I went to the closet and found crumpled notes fallen on the floor. So he found me on the floor and my notes of apology, but he didn't melt.

Sarina told me he had left for the weekend and wouldn't be back until Monday.

Day 6 – Sunday – I wanted to die in his bed.

Day 7 – Monday – I started working from home. Alia came over in the morning to hand me the files and discuss my schedule for the day and week. As I was not allowed to look continuously at the screen, I took endless calls to manage the work.

Day 8 – Tuesday – Work – work – work and sleeping pills.

Day 9 – Wednesday – I attempted to confront him in his office, so when he was in the conference room, I occupied the sofa in his office permanently. However, he didn't return to his office at all that day.

Day 10 – Thursday – I stayed home and worked.

Day 11 – Friday – Now, work too lost its charm.

Day 12 – Saturday – Sarina informed that again he had left for the weekend for some work!

Day 13 – Sunday – I called Simi and told her everything. She suggested to make up with him with sex as sex is the best way for two people to get over their issues but how to get a man in bed if he was nowhere to be found!

Day 14 – Monday – I didn't take sleeping pills and waited for him the whole night. But he didn't turn up. Was he sleeping in other room now?

Day 15 – Tuesday – I dressed in my old sloppy jeans and t-shirt and went to the office. I checked with Nadine if he was alone in his office, she confirmed. I went to the washroom, changed into a slutty lingerie, put on a long-coat over it and entered his cabin.

"Hi," I whispered as I stood by the office door.

He stiffened but didn't look up from his laptop.

"How many times do I need to apologize?" I asked sadly.

He didn't reply again.

I undid the buttons of the coat and opened it fully, "Will this help my case?"

Curiously, he looked up and rage flashed in front of his eyes.

I was about to drop the coat when he looked up quickly to the ceiling, "Cameras, damn it!" and shutting the flap angrily, he threw his laptop on the wall with a mighty force shattering it.

I pulled on the coat again and slumped by the wall, terrorized.

My whole body was shaking with fear and grief. Nadine rushed inside and saw him fuming in his seat and me cowering by the wall. She bent down and helped me get up.

"Come on, darling, come," and she dragged me outside.

Once out of his cabin, I saw everyone standing there, looking at me curiously. Gripping the buttons of my coat to protect the little dignity I had left, I ran to the bathroom, changed into my pathetic clothes and rushed outside.

I went back home and packed up my things. Everything I had brought from India was there, everything except my passport. I searched every corner of the house but could not find it. Assuming it was lost when I ran away last time, I decided to get a new one issued at the High Commission of India, London.

Luckily my dad was very thorough. He had a copy of my passport back home, so I requested him to email it to me so that I could apply for a fresh passport on its basis. Then packing up my things, I booked a 'self-driven' car like last time but couldn't get one due to lack of passport.

So faced with the worst-case scenario, I 'borrowed' one of Shaun's cars and drove myself to the High Commission of India.

They issued me some documents to show that I have genuinely lost my passport and asked me to come back in two weeks' time.

"Two weeks?" I exclaimed.

"That's the earliest. Come back with the application and we will give you the new one with your visa," the man behind the counter said and I walked out.

"Two weeks!" I sighed as I sat in Shaun's car.

I Googled for a place nearby and found 'Bexhill', a small town on the outskirts of London, and decided to live there peacefully for two weeks.

I booked a room in a small B&B in Bexhill town and drove randomly. It was around 5 PM when I arrived at Stonehenge.

I knew in normal scenario Shaun would have made fun of me for visiting the Stonehenge again, but if I had two weeks to spend in the country I was supposed to spend the rest of my life in, then at least I could visit it properly. And this time I knew he wouldn't come looking for me. He was done!

I walked around Stonehenge for an hour or so. Then sitting on the grass, I mapped out places I could visit in the next two weeks. I could then circle back to London to collect my passport, return Shaun's car and head back to India.

The thought of returning to India weighed on me more than I could imagine. I slumped to the grass and tried to hold my tears as much as possible. People around were keeping their distance from me as I was the odd one out in the company of happy travellers.

As the darkness fell around me and the crowd thinned, I too decided to make way to the town of Bexhill which now was 3 hours behind me. As I walked to my car, I saw a few men in black walking around. My heart skipped a few beats but they were just there, roaming around. Ignoring the men, I ran to my car, unlocked it and was about to close it when the other side of the car opened and a man sat beside me.

If I hadn't recognized him in a heartbeat, my heart would have stopped beating.

He was not looking at me, he was just sitting there, staring ahead. I waited for him to say something but he didn't, so I just stepped out of the car, handed the key to one of his men and started to walk away.

But quick on the uptake, Shaun rushed after me, grabbed my hand and shoved me against his car. Again, he was not speaking to me, he was just glaring at me. His security formed a wide semi-circle around us like before and turned their backs to us to give some privacy.

I tried to leave but he placed his hands on either side, locking me in the cage of his arms. The memory of the day when he had locked me like this back in office in India flashed in front of my eyes. Things were so different back then, challenging but easy!

We stood there in silence for minutes; I could feel heat emitting from his body and there was so much he wanted to say to me. I felt a strange tickle all over my body and in the moment, I felt nothing better to do than grab his face and kiss him all over. I lifted my hands and they grazed his thighs. He stiffened as he looked down at my hands that were now moving all over his body. Grinding his teeth he pulled back slightly, but I grabbed his collar and pulled him closer.

He didn't stop me this time, getting encouraged by his silence, I pulled him close and pressed my mouth on his. For the first time I felt him resist kissing me but his body loosened. I kissed him fully on the lips but he didn't reciprocate. Yes, he was not pushing me, but he was not participating either. Finally, I pulled back and exhaled, feeling defeated.

"What?" I demanded now.

He narrowed his eyes but didn't reply.

"Fine!" I fumed and pointed at the man who had the keys of the car. "You!" the man didn't turn.

"The guy who has the key to this damn car, turn around," I spoke.

The man turned, looked at us standing mere inches away and looked down.

"Take out my bag and purse from the car, please," I requested.

Without looking at us, he quickly did the needful. He placed the bag next to us and handed me my purse and turned back again.

"Now, if you will excuse me," I spoke to Shaun as I bent down to grab my bag, "I have to leave."

But he just grabbed my waist from behind and pushed me on the car and forced himself on me from behind. I felt him getting turned on as he rubbed his nose on the back of my neck.

"What is this?" he spoke finally as he placed a note and the ring he had given me for engagement in front of me.

I recognized it as the note I had left him today saying – *Today was the last straw. I Quit.*

"For a man who is a billionaire, you are not that intelligent, are you!" I snapped.

"What are you quitting?" he asked flatly. "And why did you leave this behind?" he wiggled the ring in between his fingers.

"How did you find me in the first place?" I demanded.

"You are kidding, right?" he snorted.

"I know you don't want to do anything with me, so why are you here?" I demanded again.

"For the woman who runs half my empire, and may run it fully in future, you are not quick on the uptake," he laughed sarcastically.

I wanted to ask what did he mean by 'half empire-full empire' but his breath on my neck was making me too weak in the knees.

"Sarina called my security in a state of panic, she asked me to come back immediately. She showed me the note and the ring, I knew you were still in the UK, so I asked my team to check up on you," he explained.

"And how did you find me here?" I demanded.

"You are driving a top-end Ferrari, they have built in GPS, did you know," he informed and I stared at the roof of the car I was pressed against at the moment.

"This is a Ferrari?" I asked, shocked.

"Oh yes," he spoke seductively. "Didn't you know?"

"I was in too much of a hurry to leave, I just wanted to run away," I sighed.

"Without your passport?" he smirked.

"I lost it – I will get a new one in two weeks. Hey," I turned and now he was pressing fully on me from front. I felt my whole body explode with desire for him and I felt same in him too, "how do you know –" I gulped to control myself, "how do you know I don't have my passport?"

"Because I have it," he spoke, pressing himself more firmly on me.

"What? How dare you?" I wanted to shout but in the present situation, I could hardly speak in any emotion that wasn't pure desire for him.

"My house, my rules!" he spoke, pressing his lips on my throat and swallowing my skin.

"I want my passport," I pressed his chest to push him away but instead gripped his shirt to draw him closer.

"But I want you," he muttered pushing his hand inside my shirt and tracing the lower band of my bra.

"No..." I breathed, and though my word was 'no', it sounded so much like 'yes'.

"Oh, screw that," and he opened the door of the car to push me inside when his phone buzzed.

He pulled out his phone to answer it when I pulled out a bottle of water and splashed my face. What was wrong with me? About to have sex in a public space, surrounded by eight bodyguards! Shaun sat in the car to take the call when I picked up my bag and started to walk away. Two men followed me while six stayed with Shaun. I was by the road where two cabs were still standing to take the last of the tourists away when he caught up with me.

"You have a death wish?" he asked from a distance.

"No," I turned to face him, "all my wishes are dead now."

"Will you go to Bexhill?" I asked a cab driver. He looked at the two men standing close to me and shook his head. I asked another driver, he too denied.

"Awesome," I sighed and looked for the nearest public transport.

Shaun came up to me, pulled my purse and threw it at one man and pointed another to take my bag, then hoisting me on his shoulder in a fireman's lift, he carried me back to his cars.

"You insulted me," he started.

"So did you," I shrugged.

"You slapped me," he added.

"And you addled my brain for two fucking weeks," I snapped.

"You accused me of incest," he growled.

"And for that I am sorry. In my defence, I was in immense pain and was concussed and whatnot!" I apologised.

"Hmm," he crossed his arms at this, "fair enough!"

"You ignored me, you ignored my pleas, you ignore my apologies," I added.

"I was furious," he shrugged.

"You took my passport!" I shrieked.

"So that you don't run away," he pouted. "Can't believe you applied for a duplicate," he laughed.

Feeling agitated, I demanded, "What do you want?"

"Right now?" he asked with raised eyebrows.

"From me!" I shouted.

"Sex... lots of it... like right now," he shook his head clumsily.

"I threw myself at you today and you threw your laptop at the wall," I exclaimed.

"There is a camera in my office and you know it," he gritted his teeth.

"You – we were about to have sex the day I arrived, in your office," I spoke in disbelief.

"I had unplugged it then," he growled. "Didn't I say what is underneath these clothes is only mine now!"

"Funny way of treating something that is only yours!" I rolled my eyes.

His phone buzzed again, he cursed, "Damn it, it is a weekday!"

"Yeah, and weekend was two days ago. Where the fuck were you?" I demanded.

He looked at me angrily for a second then asked, "Why are you going to Bexhill? What's there?"

"Small town, beach, peace," I shrugged.

"Hmm..." and he pulled out his phone and searched for something quick. Then using my phone to dial a number, he spoke, "I would like to book a room, name – Kaya Pradhan, the best room you have to offer."

"Sam," he said.

"Sir," the tallest of all the security spoke.

"Here," and Shaun thrust his phone in his hand. Sam looked shocked. "Kaya and I are going to spend a few days off the grid. So give us some space. You will call me only if my mother is dead, okay?"

"What?" Sam was utterly shocked.

"I need some privacy, which is very hard to come by these days," Shaun grunted.

"Where are you going, sir?" Sam asked.

"Does it matter?" Shaun looked irritated.

"We need to sweep the place for any bugs, cameras or any kind of threat, sir. Please, you know the protocol," Sam insisted.

Shaun swore then showed Sam the name of the hotel he had just booked. Sam nodded and went to other men, and within seconds four of them went away.

I felt my whole-body tickle in anticipation of what Shaun was planning. Was he really going to spend a few days with me, alone! Without his phone and laptop?

"I should have done this the day you arrived," Shaun hissed, "anyway, better late than never. Are you ready for endless bouts?"

I felt even the roots of my hair blush at these words.

"Oh, don't do that right now... do you know I have had sex only for twenty-four hours in the past ten months? I am horny beyond your imagination," he muttered pushing himself on me, "I am just gonna –" he paused, "well, I will not say, I will just show what I am gonna do to you."

And with one deep heavy exhale, he pushed me in the car and drove away.

Chapter 7

Ten minutes later we arrived at a decent looking hotel and as we stepped out of the car, his security led us straight to the room.

Two men were doing a sweep for any bugs and cameras in the room when Shaun asked Sam, "Is the bathroom clean?"

Sam looked at the other two men, who nodded and he affirmed.

Shaun showed it to me, and quietly I exited the room.

I washed my face, came out and took my bag inside the bathroom. Placing it carefully on the sink, I undressed and went into the shower. The water was barely lukewarm but still I enjoyed it.

I sat on the floor and placed my head in between my knees and let the water flow.

"What are you doing?" he asked.

"Thinking," I replied without looking up.

"Not the right time," he muttered as I heard him undress too. "I have a lot of pent-up energy that I am dying to get rid of, and finally, I have you with me."

After a minute or so, he too walked in the shower and interrupted the flow of water I was enjoying.

"It is cold," he winced.

"I know…" I groaned and looked up, shivering now.

"Remember the first time we made love," he asked, sitting in front of me.

I saw his naked body from top to toe and multiple, endless dirty things flashed through my mind.

"Okay, that's it," he spoke, grabbing my hand and lifting me in his arms he stepped out of the bathroom.

"What?" I asked, surprised.

"I want you to do all the dirty things you just thought of," he grinned as he threw me on the bed and climbed on it. "I don't think I can ever control myself when you look at me like that," and turning the lights off, he pressed his lips on my body.

♥

"Freed some energy?" I asked as I panted loudly.

"Some," he huffed too, trying to catch his breath. "I am out of practice," he complained as he fell beside me and placed his hand on my waist. I felt him trace the scar on my tummy with his finger and I felt it tingle. It had been throbbing like mad for the past hour but I didn't wince or show it, I was not going to let this pain hamper what Shaun had planned for us. If he needed to exhaust his pent-up energy, so did I. Remembering the pain-killers I had in my bag, I pushed the pain back and cherished the man who was pushing back everything just to be with me.

"Umm…" I moaned, "I don't think you should ever stop the 'practice'," I rolled and placed my head on his chest. His heart was hammering. "I missed you, you know… these two weeks, I have missed you so much."

"Me too," he kissed my head and squeezed me in his arms.

"I—" I started but he stopped me by putting his lips on mine.

"Don't – talk," he ordered as he kissed me more.

"As you command," and before he knew it, I pushed him on his back and climbed on top of him.

♥

We slept, we ate, we bathed and had sex... I didn't know how many hours we spent in the confines of the room but I was sure it was more than twenty-four hours.

We both were lying on the floor, where we had spent last thirty minutes doing vigorous activities, when my phone buzzed.

Shaun got up and glanced at the caller ID. "Unknown number," he spoke as he passed on the phone to me. I answered without any interest.

"Who is this?" I asked on speaker.

"Where is he?" a woman's voice came through.

"Again, who is this?" I demanded, though I got a hint of who it was, due to the attitude.

I heard loud tutting on the other side of the line.

"Whatever," I spoke and disconnected the call.

"That was Mia, by the way," Shaun laughed.

"I know," I laughed with him.

"By the way, I feel all sticky," I complained as I touched my own skin.

"Want me to clean it up?" he asked, sucking my stomach.

I was about to answer in the most sensuous way when the phone buzzed again.

"Who is this?" I answered.

"This is Mia, where is my damn brother?" she demanded.

Shaun shook his head.

"I don't know, he is avoiding me, isn't he?" I barked.

"Then whom are you romancing?" she asked rather crudely.

"Not your brother, now go and bother someone else," and with a snap, I disconnected the call.

I was about to move when the phone buzzed again.

"You are harshing my buzz, you know!" I spoke as I answered with a laugh.

"Are you fucking kidding me, my brother, your fiancé is missing for more than two days and you don't care!" Mia shouted.

"What?" I sat up straight and saw Shaun doodling on my inner thigh. "Two days?"

"Yes, two days. His security head is not aware of where he is. His phone is with Sam - the giant, and you are slutting around with other men..." Mia accused.

"Don't call her a slut," Shaun barked instinctively.

Dead silence! I closed my eyes as I laughed at his cuteness. In his hurry to defend me, he forgot.

"You are there, aren't you?" Mia asked through gritted teeth.

"Of course, I am here," Shaun answered.

"I thought you guys were fighting hard," Mia sounded confused.

"Yes, and we make up even harder," Shaun laughed as he slumped back in my arms and laughed. "By the way, my wife doesn't romance with anyone else but me." My body got covered in goosebumps at the word 'wife'. This change, which may have gone unnoticed if I had been dressed, didn't get missed by Shaun's eyes as we both were completely naked and wrapped around each other. He raised his eyebrows as he scanned my body with hair on their ends now. He was bending to kiss me when Mia shrieked, "Your wife! Don't tell me you ran off to some chapel and got married."

"Well, fiancée, same difference really," Shaun shrugged. "What do you want?"

"Your whereabouts to start with!" she snapped.

"Sorry, can't tell," Shaun spoke with a smug smile.

"Didn't mom instruct you to not sleep with her before the wedding?" Mia complained.

"And isn't mom asking you since your teenage years to not hand over your ass to every Tom, Dick and Harry you meet?" Shaun laughed again.

"Stop insulting me in front of strangers," Mia growled.

"Stop treating Kaya like a stranger," Shaun reasoned.

"When are you coming back from your honeymoon?" Mia tutted.

"So it is Thursday already?" Shaun wondered.

"Yes," Mia spoke exasperatedly.

"Time flew by, didn't it," Shaun snickered as he looked at me.

"Oh my God! Don't act like a teenager," Mia exclaimed.

"I will see you on Sunday, or Monday, alright?" Shaun informed.

"Go fuck yourself," Mia cursed.

"Oh, I don't need to, I have my wife here," Shaun laughed and I closed my eyes in embarrassment.

"Don't call her that," Mia spoke through gritted teeth.

"And, Mia," Shaun spoke seriously.

"What?" Mia snapped.

"Stop calling non-stop and harshing our buzz else I would be forced to dump this phone too. And I want to keep it on for real emergencies," and throwing the phone on the side, he looked down at me and spoke, "So, Kaya," he whispered seductively, "let's see what changes come over your body when I make love to you as Mrs Malani."

Chapter 8

We left the hotel room around midnight on Saturday. Shaun was not at all willing to come before Monday but I insisted. If not me, at least he needed some hours to see what happened around the globe in his multinational conglomerate.

"You know, I have never done something like this before, disappearing from the grid for days," Shaun laughed as he drove us to the house.

"Neither have I, but in your case, I am sure it must be catastrophic. I dread to see what we will find tomorrow," I shuddered.

"You do know how to 'harsh my buzz'," he mocked me.

"Did I tell you recently how much I loved you?" I asked thoughtfully.

"Actually, no… you showed it to me in the past few days, but not so much in words," and he bent down to kiss me again.

"Shaun!" I scolded as someone honked and he sat straight. "No more taking your eyes off the road."

"Buzz harsher," he pouted and drove on.

♥

"We came home early now; it took me a few hours to reach there," I commented as we entered the driveway of Airia.

"How slow do you drive?" Shaun commented, laughing still. I couldn't help but notice how happy he was, and it gave me immense pleasure that I was the source of his happiness.

"A little too slow, I presume," I said out loud.

"It's good, I want you to drive slow and safe," he spoke as he bent and kissed me again.

"Shaun!" I scolded him.

"What? No more road…" he smiled and pressed his lips on mine again.

I smiled broadly with his lips on mine and he pulled back to see my delight.

"Oh, I love you so much," he moaned. "I cannot express how much I have missed sharing this with you."

"We have a perfectly good bedroom upstairs, we can continue sharing it," I pouted.

And taking the hint, he jumped out of the car, rushed to my side and even before I could step out, he lifted me in his arms. "Let me do the honours."

The lights of the house turned on as we climbed the steps of the house, and even before we reached the main door, it was wide open.

"Oh no, what happened this time," Sarina cried.

Shaun stopped dead on his feet, looked down at my blushing face and spoke, "Well, we made up," he laughed and raced me upstairs to his bedroom, me giggling non-stop like a teenager.

I looked back at Sarina, she was blushing and smiling too. But her smile said how happy she was to see us finally together.

Shaun placed me on his bed, took off his already half dangling shirt and spoke, "Now let's christen this bed," and before I knew it, he was on top of me.

♥

When I woke up next, Shaun was sitting in bed, not with newspaper, laptop or phone, but with a bowl full of cereals and was looking down at me with warmth and affection.

"Looks like you are yet to have your fill," I smiled, sitting up as well, sheets falling from my torso.

He looked down at my bare chest and smiled, "I don't think I can ever have my fill. But I think I need to hit pause else I will kill you."

I grinned, "Not dying that easily, and I think I do want more..."

His jaw dropped at my words. "Really?" he asked, amazed. "We have barely slept in the past few days."

"We can sleep when we are old," I grinned.

"Now that's an agreement I love very much, here, have some energy," and he fed me some cereal from his bowl.

Someone knocked, and as I disappeared in the bathroom to get fresh, I heard him call, "Enter."

"Kaya," Shaun called after a minute or so.

"Yes," I replied snickering and wondering what happened to 'gaining some energy'.

"I am heading downstairs, get dressed and join me, okay?"

Did he sound serious? I quickly opened the door but he was already gone.

Wondering what could have possibly happened, I got dressed in my shorts and t-shirt, first thing I found in the bag I had packed for my travel last week, and hurried out.

There was pin drop silence in the house. I was wondering where to go in this huge house, most of which I had not yet seen due to my work, health and other issues, when I saw a butler step out of a room.

"Is he in there?" I asked the butler.

"Yes, ma'am," the butler bowed and went away.

I knocked and entered, and stopped dead on my feet. Standing by the window, dressed in an elegant magenta coloured saree was none other than Shaun's mother, *The Mrs Malani.*

She turned, saw me from head to toe and her brow furrowed. In one look I could tell that despite living abroad, her mentality was old-school. Only if he had told me, I would have dressed in something that covered me at least!

"Kaya," his mother acknowledged my presence.

"*Namaste,* aunty," and I hurried forward and bowed down to touch her feet as a sign of respect.

She placed her hand on my head and I stood back straight.

"Sit," she spoke and pointed at a sofa on which Shaun was not sitting. I sat and Shaun got up from his sofa and joined me, sitting rather close to me.

"What are you doing here, mom?" Shaun asked seriously.

"How is *maasi ji?"* I added.

"At least one of you know what to ask," his mother commented sarcastically.

"I know how she is, didn't I talk to you a few days ago?" Shaun rolled his eyes.

"Yes, a few days ago!" his mother snapped.

"What happened, mom?" Shaun asked with a sigh this time.

"This happened," and she threw a newspaper on the table in front of us. Shaun reached for and opened it. The headlines of Page 3 read – ***The Billionaire Malani runs away with his run-away fiancé***

"'Run-Away Fiancé'?" Shaun said scathingly.

"And that's what is bothering you? You went off the grid for five days. Five days, Shaun! Stock prices have taken a down turn. There is a major upheaval in day-to-day functioning. Never could I believe you would do something so stupid in your life. You run this business, millions of lives are dependent on your one move, and you *ran away!"*

I felt ashamed at these words. It was all my fault but his mother was not looking at me, she was continuously glaring at her son.

"Explain!" she ordered.

"I needed a break; don't I deserve a break?" Shaun retorted.

"Everyone needs a break, but there is a course of action that needs to be taken when a person in your position takes a break. You assign a counterpart on your behalf. Someone who can take decisions for you. Someone who can guide the world what to do when their leader is unavailable. What could be so damn important that you left your phone and laptop for five whole days?" his mother was shouting now.

Shaun didn't reply and I sat like I was carved out of stone, too scared to even move a muscle.

"I will check up on things today," Shaun sighed. "One week, I cannot get one damn week."

"No, you cannot," his mother snapped. "You should have thought about it before becoming the CEO of this bloody empire. Do you have any idea how your father worked? Did you never see him? He never took a day off, and you ran away for FIVE DAYS!"

"I know how dad worked, alright," Shaun groaned. "His all-work attitude didn't allow him too much to spend with us, did it?"

"Don't talk about your father like that," his mother shouted.

Shaun was about to say something but I placed my hand on his thigh to stop him from saying something he would regret. Shaun looked at my hand and went mute.

His mother didn't miss this gesture. She just glared at me and I could tell she was wondering how did I have such strong hold on Shaun!

"Mom, would you like to be interim CEO for a month or so?" Shaun laughed after a pause, "I could use a longer break," and gave me a quick glance.

His mother's face hardened. A small smile that had curved on my lips vanished liked a fused light bulb. I wanted to go but I was too scared to move.

"Are you an animal?" his mother asked in a threatening whisper.

"Depends on what part of my personality you are referring to," Shaun spoke so casually that my eyes popped open and my face burnt.

"You couldn't have found time to check your mails or phone?" his mother asked angrily.

"No, that's why I ditched them," Shaun shrugged.

"How could you be so relaxed about this?" his mother shouted this time.

"Because, mom, I am happy for the first time in a long time," Shaun replied.

"I am not against your happiness, but business is important as well," his mother retorted.

"I—" Shaun started but I dared myself and interjected, "I am very sorry, aunty, we both are. And it will never happen again!"

His mother gave me a sharp look and I was silenced again.

"At least one of you has some sense," his mother breathed.

Shaun laughed again and his mother's frown was back in place.

"What are you doing?" I whispered to Shaun.

"What? I don't want to make any false promises to her," Shaun replied. "I don't lie to my mother, never!"

"And is she lying to me?" his mother asked gravely.

"No, aunty, seriously. At least with me, I will ensure he will never leave his laptop or phone behind without prior arrangements," I assured.

"You—" Shaun glared at me, then added, "buzz-harsher."

"I want you, Shaun, to come back home with me, you should live there," his mother continued with her agenda.

"You mean Kaya and I?" Shaun asked.

"No, Kaya will live here, and you will live there," his mother added.

Shaun laughed, shifted, wrapped his arm around my shoulder and spoke, "Not happening."

"Then I am moving here with you," his mother threatened.

"You are most welcome, mom. But I am not moving your temple in this house and I am not moving my booze out as well. This is my party place, and my party stays here," Shaun shrugged.

"I know you consider me old-school and whatnot..." his mother began but Shaun interrupted her.

"One sec, mom," Shaun spoke and turned to me, "why don't you go."

I didn't need telling twice. I jumped to my feet, folded my hands in customary *namaste* in front of his mother, who glared at the two of us, and rushed out.

"First," she called out and I stopped and turned, "are you okay if Shaun moves back to his own room in our house? While you live here, alone."

I nodded quickly, as if there was any other option for me.

"Good, now you can go if you like," she announced and I ran out before she could stop me again.

"Mom, you are unbelievable," Shaun barked and I stopped just outside the door.

"Why? Is she too sensitive to hear my views?" his mother spoke.

"Maybe I don't want to hurt her with your old-school thoughts, that's it," Shaun spoke.

"Yes, I am old-school. Your father married a pure, traditional Indian girl and I know he too never liked my beliefs, but I can't help it. I am what I am and I didn't change for him, I won't change for you," his mother thundered.

"I know what issues you and dad had, you guys were not very quiet when you fought, alright!" he said with a hint of sadness in his voice.

"Good that you are aware then," his mother replied simply. "So I don't have to tell you what I want."

"What do you want, mom? What are you asking from me?" he spoke in a tired tone.

"I asked for no sex before marriage," his mother informed.

"I am an adult," Shaun defended.

"So I have noticed," his mother barked.

"Good," Shaun replied.

"Is your generation out of control? Can't you people wait?" his mother snapped.

"I don't know my entire generation, but I like to have sex when I want to and with the woman I want to. It is consensual, I am not committing a crime here," Shaun replied casually. And even though I was not in their company, I felt my face burn.

"Unbelievable. You were never this arrogant and deviant. What has gotten into you?" his mother continued.

"I have always been like this, you are just noticing it now, maybe," Shaun replied.

"I need a good reason else, I mean it, I will move into this house today," his mother threatened. My hair stood on their ends at the thought of knowing his mother would be around while Shaun and I slept in the same bed!

"Because," Shaun sighed finally, "I will not abandon her ever again. I will not make her go through what she went through with her ex-husband."

My heart got heavy at the mention of Daksh, my ex. Daksh was a good man, he still is and I still felt guilty with what went down between us.

"Oh right, she was married. She has been with other man."

Her tone was so contemptuous that I felt offended, and so did Shaun because he replied, "Please keep your judgment to yourself, mom. She has been with one man who was her legal husband. Whereas your bachelor son has been with hundreds of women before. And not to mention your own unmarried daughter who may have been with a thousand of men till date."

A ringing silence met these words, and I didn't know what was passing between the mother-son duo. *A hundred and a thousand?* Was this brother-sister combo walking sex-machine?

Shaun sighed after a long pause and spoke, "Don't you think it is better that I have been with one woman a hundred times than a hundred different women?"

"You both – I mean – a hundred times already?" his mother was flabbergasted.

"Well, when you are locked in a room for straight five days, you lose count after a while," Shaun laughed carelessly and tears of humiliation escaped my eyes.

Another silence!

"Listen, mom," Shaun now spoke with finality, "I love her. I really do. She is the one. And I know you are old-school and have orthodox thoughts but we are adults. We have freewill. We will live the way we want, love the way we want and do everything the way we want. I will assure you one thing though, we will not have kids until we are legally married, okay? Because that's one scandal I too want to stay away from."

"Why wait for having kids too? Have that scandal as well then," his mother barked.

"Well, if it happens, it may but I deliberately do not want to put a lid on my pleasure train just yet," Shaun spoke thoughtfully.

"What are you people? Animals?" his mother asked in shock.

"We are young, mom. Young and free. Now what would you like to have for breakfast?" and I heard Shaun's footsteps approaching the door, and I ran, as fast I could, upstairs so that they did not catch me overhearing.

Chapter 9

His mother left after having breakfast, which I conveniently skipped by faking sleep. I knew I would have to face her in future, but I would prefer to keep that future at a certain distance as long as possible.

Shaun spent most of the Sunday working in his home office. I too had some work to catch up on but I didn't. I just called Simi, my brother and my parents to chat and discuss their lives. While I was overhearing Shaun and his mother, I realized that I had been ignoring my family ever since I came here. They understood how much work I had but still it was no excuse and I decided to call them more frequently.

"Finally free?" I asked Shaun as he entered the room at around 4:30 in the afternoon.

"Not yet!" he sighed as he walked in the closet and pulled out fresh clothes. "Video conference," he added.

"Take a shower at least," I commented as he undid his bottom.

"You know this all is your fault," he scowled.

"What did I do?" I retorted.

"I knew I would be busy the day I return, that's why I wanted to come back tomorrow," he complained.

"When will you be free? I want to talk to you," I started.

He considered me for a moment, then checked the clock. "Have a call in ten minutes," he pouted. "What do you want to discuss."

"Will take more than ten minutes I am sure," I spoke thoughtfully.

"Hmm..." he spoke grabbing my legs and dragging me off the bed.

"What are you doing?" I asked, surprised.

"You are filthy too, let's take a very quick ten-minutes shower, *together,*" and hoisting me on his shoulder, he headed to the bathroom.

♥

I was at the dinner table when he joined me.

"Finally, done," he groaned. He was visibly tired.

"Who was shouting just now?" I asked seriously.

"Ron, the one who manages Australia. He was in another mess and needed me, but well, I wasn't there," he shrugged.

The name Ron reminded me of something. "He is the one who called you when we were together in India?" I asked.

"Yep, that's the one..." Shaun nodded, looking disgusted.

"But you said he is like you best friend..." I added curiously.

"And?" he spoke without any interest.

"Not the way one usually refers to when talking about 'best friend'," I pointed and he grimaced.

"I think you missed the sarcasm when I had said 'he was like my best friend.' Ron and I don't see eye to eye, like ever. He usually messes up and expects me to clean up afterward," he sighed.

"Oh..." and I trailed off remembering the day and conversation.

"And I may go to South Africa tomorrow evening," he added, "I think Ron is going to follow me there this time," he finished grudgingly.

"Oh, alright," my face fell at the words.

"I would have asked you to join me, but thanks to your filing for new passport, your old passport is cancelled," he made a face.

"Hey, blame yourself for hiding the fact you 'stole' my passport," I complained.

"Only insurance to ensure you don't run away," Shaun elaborated. "It is easier to follow you to Stonehenge in comparison to India. By the way, you really loved Stonehenge, didn't you?"

I shrugged this time.

"Two visits in a month, too much love for a couple of stones, isn't it?" he remarked.

"I knew you would say something like this. The first time I visited for sightseeing but we ended up fighting, and the second time, well I was way too hurt and heartbroken and didn't know where to go. So I ended up where our fight began," I replied morosely.

His expressions softened at my words.

"I am sorry," he spoke.

"Me too," I added.

"Don't mind me asking, but I always thought you had 'fight and no flight' attitude. Now, why do you always want to run away?" he asked, concerned.

I sighed. I knew what he meant. Ever since I have met him, things have been dramatically different.

"This… our life… our relationship is complicated," I started.

"I am sorry for bringing this up, but your old life was complicated; this, us, is simple. I love you, more than anything in this whole God-damn world… and yet, your first instinct is always to run away from me," he sighed.

"Daksh and I were friends before…" I spoke. He was about to retort but I raised my hand so that he allows me to finish. "Daksh and I knew each other for more than fifteen years. We were together in school, in college, at work… he is, I mean, he was my best friend. Even before we got engaged, he was my safety net…"

Shaun stared at me with incomprehensible expressions.

"I love you, Shaun… so damn much that it hurts me physically. The thought of staying away from you even for a moment pains me in my chest," I pressed my hand on my heart as it felt very heavy at the moment. "But I have endured so much recently, so much has changed in my life… I feel alone here. I know I have you, but I left my entire world when I came here… I am sorry, but for now, whenever something happens between us, my first instinct is to go back. Not to Daksh, never to him… but to Simi, my dad, my brother…"

"So, I am not your safety net?" Shaun looked heart-broken.

"You are my home," I heaved a sigh, "you are my safety net, my everything. But sometimes, a lot of times these days, I feel I am getting entangled in my own safety net. Do you know what I mean?"

"I actually don't," he looked at me with quizzical expressions.

"I don't know how to explain," I shrugged.

"Explain me this then, when would you stop thinking about running away from me? When would you start trusting me as much, if not more, as you trusted *him?*" he demanded and I stared at him, baffled.

"I trust you more than I trusted Daksh. Do you think, otherwise I would be here? But I know what you mean. Would you give me some time to adjust here? I think, with time, I will start feeling at home here. And then, my first instinct would not be to run to my house in India, but coming here… whenever shit would go down."

"You drive me crazy, woman," he spoke as he jabbed his fork in my direction.

"Crazy is what you fell in love with, isn't it?" I grinned.

"That is true," he shrugged and smiled. "Anyway, what did you want to talk about?" he asked as he put a morsel in his mouth.

"Let's first finish our meal as it may upset you," I commented.

He stopped in the middle of his bite, "Will your 'more than ten minutes' conversation upset me? Of course, I know it would, especially, on the day my mother ambushed us. So feel free to speak!"

"Speaking of your mother, is she really coming to live here?" I asked seriously.

He almost choked on his food as he laughed at my tone. "Fret not, she is already on a plane to California. She came back because Mia created a scene that I had disappeared, but she had to go back. *Maasi ji* is not well, you know old age and all. Mom won't leave *maasi* alone for long."

"Okay," I smiled wondering if his *maasi* being sick was a boon or a curse! "But I have to live with her and Mia when we officially marry, isn't it?"

He looked at me for a moment, then shook his head. "We can live here permanently if you like," he pointed around the house with his fork. "I anyway have lived half my life in this house, away from home. Mom doesn't allow alcohol in the mansion, you see. She has her 'God' there!"

"Mansion?" I asked.

"Yes, that's what it is called. It looks like a castle, but its name is 'Mansion'," he informed.

"Okay," I sighed, "so when you used to live here, did you bring your ex-girlfriends here as well?" I asked suddenly and he choked again.

"Err—" he hesitated.

"Oh my God!" I exclaimed.

"Never in our bedroom, though," he raised his hands in defence. "The only naked woman that room has seen is you," he added.

"And that's supposed to comfort me?" I asked with narrowed eyes. "And you saying to your mother that I have been with only one other man before you, but you have been with hundreds of women before me!"

This time he literally paused. "You heard that?" he asked.

"I heard everything, I didn't leave," I informed.

"You eavesdropper," he accused with a laugh.

"Who talks to his mom like this? Sex animal, lidding the pleasure train, hundred times in closed room, yuck! You have no shame or boundaries?" I scolded.

"Well, I don't lie to mom," he shrugged and started eating again. "And I do have boundaries, but some conversations just create confusions when we stay in boundaries. I just told her I won't stop having sex with you just because she is old-school."

I just gawked at him so he added, "Right, your mom is old-school too."

"I would prefer if you maintained boundaries with your mother," I finished.

"Even if it means lying to her?" he asked with raised eyebrows. I didn't reply to this.

"Would you tell our children to not have sex before marriage and hide it from you?" he asked very seriously.

"I may tell them that. Afterall I was a virgin before I got married," I crossed my arms.

"Yeah, and you were almost a virgin when you met me," he laughed but stopped at the look on my face.

Frowning at his comment, I quickly finished my meal and left the table. He followed me soon after.

"Do I need to de-virginize you again to uplift your mood?" he asked as he found me in the library I had just discovered in the house. I didn't know he had such a huge collection of Classic novels. I was mesmerized.

"I wish to read to uplift my mood," I commented without looking at him.

"Oh, please don't be like this," he spoke, nibbling at my ear. "I am sorry, okay? I promise to behave myself in front of my mom."

I exhaled.

"And, no, I have not been with a hundred women before you. I exaggerated to make my point. And I am sure Mia has not been with a thousand men. But see, it helped my case, didn't it?" he explained.

"So technically you lied to your mother while you claim you don't lie to her ever," I spoke and he glared at me.

"There is a difference. I don't know exact numbers so I just said hundred. Should I call Sam and ask for a number? I can tell you exactly how many women have rolled with me in bed naked," he barked.

I snapped the book I was pretending to read shut and went back to the room.

"You are horrible. Should I tell you how many times I have rolled in bed naked with my ex-husband? What all I have done with him? At least mine was with my husband at the time, but you!" I shouted.

He fisted his fingers angrily.

"He was impotent," he retorted.

"He was uninterested after I fell sick. He was very romantic and passionate at the beginning of our marriage," I growled.

Shaun fumed with rage while I stared at him.

"Don't repeat that ever again," he threatened.

"Same to you, do you have any idea what I went through when that girl answered your cell? How many scenarios rolled in front of my eyes of you with other women," I raged.

"That was not my cell," he corrected.

"Then did you stop to think who added that fake number in my phone under your name? I had called you the day before and the number was correct. But from the day you went away, it changed. Did you stop to think that maybe someone is trying to sabotage us?" I shouted.

"I got that number checked, it was a burner. And it must be a mistake," he shrugged.

"The girl said, and I remember quite well, '*It is your Kaya. Shaun, I mean, Mr Malani cannot come to the call right now...*'"

Shaun frowned at these words, "Must be someone's practical joke!"

"Joke or strategy to break us up?" I asked calmly this time.

Shaun approached me at these words and rubbed my arms, "Is it so easy to break us up?" he asked.

"I don't know, you tell me?" I spoke as I grabbed his collar and tugged at it.

"Don't you trust me at all?" he asked, his eyes burning hot with pain.

"I trust you and I am sorry for ever doubting you," I sniffed. I felt deeply ashamed for ever thinking he would cheat on me.

"I would never cheat on you, can you believe that?" he added.

"Even if I saw you kissing another woman, I won't," I smiled.

"Oh really?" he asked with raised eyebrows, "What if someone pushed me in her bed and pretended to have sex with me?"

"I won't believe it," I shook my head at his childishness.

He grinned broadly at these words.

"Let's make a deal then," I suggested.

"What?" he spoke as he wrapped his arms around me and squeezed me against his firm body.

"Till the time we say, 'yes, I cheated on you', we won't believe otherwise. No matter what we see, what we hear, we will trust each other."

"Deal," he smiled and bent to kiss me.

"Always remember our deal, okay," I insisted, pulling back.

"When have I ever forgotten a thing you ever said?" he asked, smiling. "What's bothering you?" he asked with concern.

"I don't belong to your world. I am an outsider and well – " But before I could continue, he pressed his lips on mine again and spoke, "You are not an outsider, you live in my heart, so in my world, you are the only person who matters, okay?"

Chapter 10

Shaun left for South Africa next evening without any comments on when he would be back. I missed him terribly and after spending so many days wrapped up together, I felt my bed exceptionally cold. But I was helpless. My passport was still a week away, despite Shaun's attempt to fast-track it, and I was stuck here.

"Maybe we should get officially married to get you a British passport," he suggested as he was getting dressed that day for his flight.

I just stared at him in shock.

"Ah, are you getting all goosebumpy again?" he laughed, tickling me.

"No," I replied, blushing.

"I am going to miss you, you know," he shook me in his arms.

"Not more than I would," I smiled sadly. "The bed would be cold without you in it."

"Hmm…" he spoke as he stared at the well-made bed, "I can warm it up for you for tonight at least." And without listening to any of my protests that he would be late, he pushed me into the bed muttering *I am the boss, you know!*

♥

With Shaun away I focused entirely on my work, which was piling up. Though, according to the label, I was 'Chief Marketing Officer' of the Malani Group, I had not taken up that role in full capacity. And in his absence, I decided to act upon it.

I started interacting with marketing teams of various brands owned by Malani Group and understanding the requirements to boost growths.

Each interaction proved one thing to me, they didn't respect me as a leader yet, but they feared me for sure. And I decided to work hard to the level that they started seeing me as their leader one day and began respecting me.

I had spent three whole days with various teams when Mia came to pay me a visit.

"I hear you are trying hard to jingle with the dud crowd. Why? Are you missing your friends and family?" she mocked me.

"Yes, I miss my friends and family," I replied coolly. "And they are not dud crowd. Every single employee of Malani Group is important to me and I do consider them as friends and family."

"Even though they call you a gold digging slut?" she asked with raised eyebrows.

I shrugged at her comment and she frowned. I now knew all too well to not react to her barking. As I focused on the file in my hand, she leaned forward and hissed, "The office in which you are so proudly sitting was supposed to be someone else's."

My head jerked up at these words.

"You have displeased a lot of people, believe me *a lot of people,* by getting your name up on that door," she pointed at the door at which it read 'Kaya Malani – Chief Marketing Officer'.

"Are you threatening me or warning me?" I asked sceptically.

She snorted loudly. "I don't like you, Kaya," she laughed.

"I know as much," I replied wondering why she was rubbing it in my face.

"But I love my brother who loves you," she sighed loudly, "You make him happy and I have seen his mood swinging with you."

I just stared at her with confused expressions, unsure of where she was going with this discussion.

"He told me what happened between you two," she informed.

My jaw dropped. Did Shaun really tell her what I accidentally accused him of? *Incest?* A sudden fear for my life gripped me.

"He may consider someone feeding wrong number under his name in your phone as a practical joke, but I don't," she shook her head dismissively. "He doesn't believe that someone would hurt him deliberately. But he is so blinded by your love and presence, that he forgets that hurting you, or driving a wedge between you two is the ideal way of hurting him!"

I was dumbfounded by her words.

"My brother is insanely in love with you, and I hate you even more for it," she scowled.

"Why?" I blanched.

"Because you have made him vulnerable and you have no idea what vulnerability can do to people like Shaun," she replied thoughtfully.

"So what are you saying?" I asked, hoping to conclude her warnings.

"Beware of what you do and whom you trust. I know it will be hard for you to believe, but I maybe the only well-wisher you may have in this country, well, except for your sex-buddy," she rolled her eyes and this time I snorted with laugh.

"Laugh all you want but I love Shaun more than you can imagine. He is not just my brother, he is my whole family. And I will be damned to see him get hurt because a slut like you broke his heart!" And with one shrewd warning look, she left.

Chapter 11

When I informed Shaun about my conversation with Mia that night, he roared with laughter.

"Ignore her, she is way too dramatic," he laughed again.

"Can I confess something?" I dared.

"Anything," his voice was full of love on phone.

"All this time I thought she was the one sabotaging our relation, you see, considering she hates me," I whispered.

"She doesn't hate you," he dismissed casually.

"Oh, she does, I am sure of it. But she loves you more, so I think I am safe," I laughed too.

"She will get over it and all will be fine. Don't worry about her and her warnings," he sighed.

"Yeah, right!" I lied. "By the way who was supposed to be CMO before me?" I asked, intrigued.

"There were four contenders, Shaurya was the acting CMO on trial basis before you but he was already informed, even before I came to India last year, that he would not be holding the position permanently. He was not able to handle the job," he informed.

"Am I able to perform?" I asked, worried.

"Do you know the names of all the brands we have?" he asked seriously.

"Of course, what a stupid question," I rolled my eyes.

"Well, Shaurya didn't even know all the brands' names despite holding the position for six months. So believe me, there is no comparison whatsoever," he laughed again.

"When are you coming back?" I asked after a while.

"I have a surprise for you," he replied and I beamed with happiness. "But don't get your hopes up, me coming back would depend on the meeting tomorrow."

"Okay, not getting my hopes up," and keeping my fingers crossed, I prayed to sleep in his arms tomorrow night.

♥

The next day he didn't come but a surprise did arrive on my phone.

A message from Shaun on WhatsApp, even though he didn't use the messaging system and used only old-school text messages for communication.

Shaun - Hi love, surprise!

Me – You, on WhatsApp?

And I triple checked his number to ensure it was not another trap. It was his personal number.

Shaun – Yes, just for you. Something happened to my text messages, they are not going through, so thought of finally crossing the bridge and installing WhatsApp!

Me – What happened to your texts?

Shaun – Don't know. Will figure it out… Anyway, let's keep this WhatsApp thing private, just between the two of us, okay!

Me, feeling elated, replied – *Your wish is always my command, sir.*

Shaun – And you will be rewarded heavily for obeying.

I snickered.

Shaun – Don't take WhatsApp's name in front of anyone, okay? Not even when we are alone, in case someone hears. I really don't want to waste hours talking and chatting with others, okay?

Me – Okay! Will you be back tomorrow?

Shaun – Considering it is weekend, hopefully I will see you tomorrow. I love you.

Me – Love you so much more.

I rechecked the number on WhatsApp and felt ecstatic.

I called him immediately and he answered on the second ring, "I know I am not supposed to talk about it, but I loved the surprise."

"Shhh..." he shushed me. "Even our walls have ears," he laughed.

"I am very happy today, and I can't wait to see you tomorrow," I beamed on his confirmation.

"So you will use it, right?" he asked gingerly.

"Oh, all the time," I laughed.

"Perfect," and laughing even loudly, he disconnected the call.

His happiness was so contagious that I felt a rush of warmth and delight in my heart.

Chapter 12

Shaun came the next day and so did my passport, much to our relief.

As he studied it, he spoke, "Did you give my proposal a thought?"

"Which one?" I asked, working on a presentation that I was supposed to present to him on Monday.

"Officially becoming Mrs Malani," he asked.

I paused, looked at the beautiful ring sitting on my finger and smiled, "I don't think your mother will be all too pleased if we didn't do a proper ceremony."

"Well, neither would be yours, but do you care?" he asked.

"I do, actually," I pouted.

He fell back in the bed annoyed and asked, "How long?"

"Not long," I smiled again. "By the way, Daksh is getting engaged and he called today to invite."

"I am not going to attend his wedding or engagement," he frowned. "I haven't forgotten he broke your face."

I winced at the memory... the day Daksh had seen the photos of me kissing Shaun in Australia he had hit me squarely on the face.

"And I broke his heart, so all is even, okay!" I scolded, "And he has invited *me,* not us."

He looked even more annoyed now. "You wish to go?" he asked seriously.

"I do, but I know it won't be wise," I sighed.

"You should go, I would love to read next day's headlines then," he mocked as he raised his hand to demonstrate headlines, "Malani's fiancée returns to India to disrupt ex-husband's engagement. What is happening with the billionaire brat!" he laughed.

"Not funny," I scolded. "And you don't need to insist like this, you know you just have to ask me only once," I smiled, smitten.

"Oh really?" he asked with raised eyebrows.

"Your wish is my command, remember," I blushed.

His eyebrows arched even higher this time. "I wish you close your laptop and come to me and collect your reward for obeying my command," he spoke seriously.

"Heavily?" I asked, licking my lips.

"Oh, let me show you the exact weight," and he pulled me in his arms.

♥

Technically I was the CMO of the Malani group, but I was not part of board meetings. Mainly because these board meetings comprised of all the existing top tiers of the Malani group and some were still less accepting of me. Shaun always insisted I joined, but given I felt they were a sort of hostile group, I witnessed it when I attended one remotely from India, I had decided to skip them for now.

"*Are you not done yet?*" I sent a WhatsApp to Shaun.

He didn't reply so I guessed the meeting was still going on! He called me after a while.

"What is my precious doing?" he smiled with love.

"Waiting for messages on WhatsApp!" I replied.

"Gosh! You are just like all others, wasting all your time on WhatsApp. It is always better to pick up the phone and call the person if you have time to waste on the stupid app!" he replied derisively.

"Like you just did," I replied, feeling a bit confused.

"Exactly," and he laughed.

"I will see you later then?" he asked seriously.

"Sooner, hopefully," I sighed and disconnected.

Though our offices were two doors away, our work schedule, especially his, didn't allow us to interact as often as people would assume. But his words bothered me. I knew he hated WhatsApp, but he chatted with me on the same as well!

Was it really him? Chatting with me? Panicking, I wrote, *"I want to see you sooner, but I know you won't be able to come. So I am going for a coffee and a scone at the place we went last weekend in ten minutes, just to refresh those memories* 😉 *"*

And I left the office knowing all too well that if it was Shaun, then he would come, despite what meetings he had.

As I waited for him, dread filled my heart.

Ten minutes!

Fifteen minutes!

Twenty minutes!

I sat there for more than thirty minutes, but he didn't come.

I was about to leave when I saw him step out of his car, talking to somebody very seriously on phone. He lifted his finger to ask me to wait and my heart swelled with relief and love.

I quickly ordered his favourite coffee for him while I stared at him. He was strolling outside. His security team was exceptionally edgy as they were continuously scanning the area.

"Yes, you heard right," he was saying when he entered the coffee shop. "Yes, tomorrow!" he bent down to kiss me on my cheek. "Have another call set up when you are done. Yes, tomorrow!" and he disconnected.

"You came!" I beamed.

"You doubted," he laughed. "I know I am late, but I would always come. You should know that."

"Why do you think I messaged you in the first place," I snickered.

"You are very naughty," he teased as he sipped his coffee.

"Many meetings today?" I asked as I stared at him affectionately.

"Why? You want me to cancel them?" he grinned.

I pouted so he added, "Urgh, you are forcing me to cancel everything!"

"Oh, no… don't worry. I will see you tonight," I beamed with a wink.

"I am flying to Brazil in the morning, so I think I *will* see you tonight," he spoke as he finished his coffee and stood up. "No scone?" he asked.

"Already had one," I shrugged, getting up too.

"Care to join me tomorrow to Brazil? But I must warn you, Mia is coming with me," he spoke as we sat in his car together.

"Your sister's hatred aside, no, I am yet to get my visa, and yes, I will get my British passport someday too," I laughed.

He pulled me closer and kissed me, "I hope you make that someday sooner," he whispered in my ears.

"Me too," I groaned as he kissed me again.

♥

Shaun left, for around a week this time, and sleeping all alone in his bed made me resolve to get that damn passport sooner.

"I am thinking of marrying Shaun, dad," I informed my father.

"When?" he asked in a straightforward tone.

"How soon can you guys come down here?" I asked.

"It is not wedding season, there will be no *muhurat*," my mother spoke from behind.

"I don't care for *muhurat* and all anymore," I sighed, "I just want to get married and be done with it!"

"Why, is he cheating on you? Are you pregnant?" my mother gasped.

"What? No, mom… it's just that we want to make it official," I lied. I simply could not tell them I wanted to get married so I could stay with him each and every night.

"You are staying in different rooms, aren't you?" my mother demanded.

"It is 6 in the morning right now, should I show you my room to ensure he is not sleeping in my bed!" I replied. Well, I was not lying at the moment.

"Get married when the time is right, you don't want to take bad omens," my mother sighed.

"We did everything right the last time, what happened to your omens then?" my father asked.

"Fine," my mother snapped. "Do whatever you feel like!"

"We already applied for visa and have got our passports stamped. We can come whenever you ask us to. Just give us one week's time to do some shopping for your wedding," my father informed.

"Err… dad! We want to do a court marriage and not –"

"Kaya Pradhan!" my mother shrieked, "*Phere, mantra, mangalsutra*, do you have no values for them?"

"Actually no, mom!" I shrugged.

"But his mother," my mother hissed, "said she wants proper ceremonious wedding. I thought at least something would happen right in your Shaun's family," she spat at his name and a wave of anger rose in me.

"Shaun will be back from Brazil next week. Can you come then? We will have some kind of wedding over the next weekend," I continued.

"Okay, we will book flight tickets," my father agreed.

"But..." my mother started but stopped abruptly. I was sure my father must have shushed her.

"Tell me the dates, I will plan your flights. And I hope you will come a little early or stay back, please," I requested.

"Why? Won't you go on your honeymoon right after?" It was my brother who spoke from behind. I blushed at the word 'honeymoon'.

"I don't think a guy like Shaun waits for honeymoon," my mother muttered.

"MOM!" I shrieked, embarrassed, "And no, we are not dying to go on our honeymoon. We will go when he will get time, which he often doesn't!"

"Too bad, sis," my brother laughed.

"I will see you then soon?" I asked hopefully. "I will book Simi's tickets on the same day as yours, so confirm soon."

"Okay," my father assured and disconnected.

Feeling relieved and super excited, I called Simi to tell her the news.

"Too early, Kaya," she drooled over the phone when she answered.

"I am getting married next week," I informed and there was dead silence. "Did you fall asleep again?" I asked, staring at my phone to check if it was still connected.

Aaaaaaahhhhhhhhhhhhhhhhhhhhhhhhhhhhhhhh!!!! She shouted. "Oh my God! On my God! Oh my God!" and I could hear her jumping.

"Wow, geez, relax," I spoke, laughing with her.

"How can I? You are marrying *The SHAUN MALANI*. I cannot relax. *Ooye,* I am yet to get a visa."

"Get it then, like today," I ordered.

"I will," she assured, "don't you dare get married without me, okay," she threatened.

"Don't you dare miss my last and final wedding, okay?" I laughed.

"He must be so happy, isn't it?" Simi asked, happiness pouring out of each syllable.

"I am yet to tell him so don't tell anyone as of now, okay?" I snickered.

"What?" she asked, shocked.

"I had to ask dad first. And he is in Brazil, anyway. If I told him I am ready to get married, he would drop everything and come down to hoist me to the altar," I blushed.

"You guys are doing it, isn't it?" she asked sceptically. "You are not acting like 'sex after marriage' kind of crap, right?"

"What has sex to do with this?" I rolled my eyes.

"Just trying to understand his hurry," she smirked.

"Maybe it is love!' I replied.

"Oh, your love makes me gag sometimes," and she made retching sounds.

"How was Daksh's engagement?" I asked. "Is the girl good?"

"It was good. She is fine. Decent and beautiful. She will keep him happy," she spoke thoughtfully. I didn't know what I felt at this news. I had no feelings for Daksh whatsoever, and technically I moved on first, but still, seeing my ex-husband with someone else felt a little eerie. I wondered how Daksh felt seeing me with Shaun, worse than this I was sure, considering we were still married when that happened!

"Are you there?" she asked.

"Yes, I am here," I spoke, shaking off the feelings.

"He was asking for you, you know. At his engagement," she added. "A part of him hoped you would come, you know, as friends."

"I wanted to, but Shaun said it would be scandalous," I informed.

"What scandal," she asked curiously.

"Malani's fiancée returns to India to disrupt ex-husband's engagement. What is happening with the billionaire brat!'" I repeated Shaun's words and Simi laughed.

"He is not wrong, you know. This would have happened, given how frequently your husband and his family feature in news headlines."

"I know, right! I never noticed these names before, but now 'Malani' name appears in some or other newspaper across globe on a daily basis," I sighed.

"Soon you will start making headlines too," Simi snickered, "I just hope in good way."

"I do too, seriously! Anyway, I have a meeting to get to, see you later and get that visa, okay," I ordered strictly.

"Sure, babe. Love you and congratulations," and she disconnected.

♥

The next few days I spent my every free second planning the wedding. First thing I did was find a beautiful but elegant wedding dress. David, who was still driving me around, sensed what I was planning and helped me find best places to look for wedding stuff.

I wanted to be 100% ready before Shaun arrived in a few days. I wanted to surprise him.

However, another surprise arrived for me on Friday afternoon.

Shaun WhatsApped me -

Shaun – Go home now.

Me – Why?

Shaun – It is a surprise.

Me – I have a meeting in 30 minutes.

Shaun – What happened to my wish, your command?

Me – Sigh! Sigh! Fine, my lord.

And cancelling my meetings for the day, I headed home only to find a big box sitting on the bed.

"What?" I laughed as I opened it. It had a key card for a hotel and a dress and some very fluffy pair of handcuffs. No, not a dress, but a very slutty piece of semi-nude lingerie. There was also a note in the box. I read it with raised eyebrows – *Miss you terribly, 6:30 PM sharp, Suite C on 6th floor. You, me, and just the contents of the box.*

I looked at the clock, it was 4 PM already. I took a shower and put on the lingerie with quite some difficulty. As I put it on, I realized what a shitty dress it was. Though it was coming down to my thigh, it had no underwear or space to wear underneath it. Wondering what had gotten into Shaun and why he was making me wear such a yucky and uncomfortable dress, I wore another dress on top of it and made my way to the hotel.

I asked David and my security team to stay downstairs and send Shaun right up, and made my way to the sixth floor. I was on my way when I saw another message pop from Shaun on WhatsApp. It was an image. I downloaded it as I entered the room and my eyes popped open at it.

"Oh my God! Shaun!" I exclaimed loudly as I stared at the photo for a few minutes. It was of a girl in similar lingerie as I was wearing under my dress and coat and the girl's hands were tied to the either side of bed with the pair of handcuffs. I gulped.

The words underneath the photo read - *I want to find you like this.*

"What has gotten into you?" I muttered as I took off my coat and dress and stood in the lingerie. I felt bare but I knew it was just due to the photograph on my phone. I looked around, the room looked clean and safe.

I placed the handcuff on my hand and tried to tie it to the bed, but the pit in my stomach didn't allow me. I took off the cuffs and threw them on the bed, "Tie me yourself, if you like," I huffed.

Feeling exceptionally uncomfortable, I turned off the lights and slipped under the sheet of the bed, heart thudding nonstop. And as the clock showed 6:30, I heard him swipe his key on the door and enter.

"I have been waiting for you," I spoke lovingly as he stepped in the room. I waited eagerly for him, but the moment lights flickered on, my heart thudded to a stop.

It was not him! It was someone else…

Chapter 13

A Few Minutes Later.

Everything was burning... my body felt like it was literally broken. I didn't know a few minutes could ruin me to my core. The man was on top of me and there was searing pain in my whole body. His breath was heavy with alcohol fumes and it was making me nauseous, but I couldn't move. He was grinning toothily, as if he was not raping me against my will but was touching me for my pleasure.

"Please... Shaun, help me...! Please...! Stopppp...!" I cried, trying again to push him.

"No one is coming, darling," the man simpered but at that moment, the door flung open and Shaun barged into the room. As my eyes fell on him, relief washed all over my body. He was here... and he was looking angry beyond comprehension. I could see his heaving chest under all that clothing.

"Shaun!" I raised my hand for him. He looked at the scene and rushed forward to pull the man cuddling me.

"Shaun!" I croaked, tears flooding my face.

"Get out now," the stranger, who just stood back, roared.

Shaun grabbed the man by his collar and punched him. The man raised his fist to hit Shaun back but Sam was already there with his men and was dragging the man out.

"Shaun," I jumped out of the bed and ran into his arms.

There were many people in the room now and I was super-aware of my semi-nakedness, but I just couldn't care. "Oh

Shaun!" I cried heavily. He didn't hug me back. He didn't console me. Someone picked up a sheet and put it on my back to cover me but Shaun didn't hug me back!

I heard commotion in the room and then after a while someone spoke, "We found two cameras and one network jammer, sir. The room is clean now."

Shaun nodded, and as the door closed, he stepped back.

"Shaun?" I croaked but he was not the same man I loved, instead, wearing the mask of his face, there was someone else staring at me with eyes full of hatred.

He raised his hand and I flinched.

"SHAUN!" The man who had covered me with the sheet screamed. Shaun fisted his hand, squinted his eyes in rage, and grabbing a nearby vase he smashed it on the wall. Splinters of the broken china hit me and I shrieked. But he didn't stop there. He roughly ran his hands through his hair and looked around like a mad man. Reaching towards the long table that had a phone, ashtray and few other items on it, he banged it so hard it overturned shattering and scattering the contents.

"Shaun…" I started to move towards him, but his body jerked with revulsion. His sudden movement shocked me and in an attempt to protect myself from getting hit I staggered back hastily landing on the bed.

"Shaun, she is not worth it," Mia spoke as she grabbed Shaun's shoulders. She had the most disgusted expression on her face.

Shaun was holding a silver object and it seemed he wanted to throw it at me.

What was happening? Why was he acting like this? Didn't he understand what had just happened!

I tried to catch his eyes but he furiously threw the silver object in my direction. It hit the bedpost heavily, missing me by a few inches.

I didn't know what hurt me most; his intention to hit me, his hatred or the fact that he had just pulled another man groping me and he didn't care.

"Why?" he growled like a wild animal in pain.

I sat up. The other man in the room handed me my coat. Quietly, I put it on.

"Because she is what she is, a slut! That's why I said you should find someone of our standard!" Mia barked.

"Shaun? What?" I asked, tears filling my eyes.

"You couldn't wait a week for me? You had to go and do this... one week... you couldn't control yourself for one week?" he snarled.

"What?" I asked, shocked.

"I can't believe it, you cheated on Daksh with me, and now you are cheating on me with that pig!" Shaun pulled at his hair.

"I am not cheating on you?" I spoke, feeling dizzy. My head and my body was pounding with everything that had just happened but this needed my attention.

"You are a slut!" Shaun barked.

"I am not cheating on you, I would never cheat on you," I tried to explain.

"Yeah, right!" Mia snickered.

"Believe me, Shaun. I would never..." I started but the other man in the room spoke, "Kind of difficult to believe when we saw you in other man's bed, isn't it?"

"That was our pact, isn't it? Even when we see the other in someone else's bed, we would ask, and we would believe," I reminded Shaun.

"What kind of deal is this?" the man asked.

"Who are you?" I demanded.

"Daniel, his friend," the man introduced.

"Shaun..." I addressed him but he was not looking at me. "Look at me," I insisted.

He looked and there was hatred and pain in his eyes.

"Remember our deal, remember our promise to each other. We will always trust each other," I spoke softly.

Mia tutted derisively.

"This is over!" Shaun whispered.

"He tried to rape me!" I pointed at the door and Shaun froze at the word. "I told him he had come to the wrong room... and he tried to rape me... you know I was waiting for you, you were late, he came instead. And you are accusing me of cheating!" I shouted.

"What is she saying?" Mia demanded.

"You knew I was in Brazil," Shaun spoke through gritted teeth. "I told you I land at 10, you knew I was not here, hence you planned this, isn't it?"

"What?" I asked, confused. "YOU CALLED ME HERE!" I shouted.

"She is a slut, bro. Let's go," Mia pulled at Shaun's arm.

Shaun let Mia drag him but I grabbed his other hand. "Wait!" I begged.

He pushed me so hard that I fell on the ground.

Daniel was beside me instantly, but I just sat there. Shaun was at the door when I said, "Shaun," I called out angrily. Shaun paused and turned, he had tears in his eyes. "I am saying this one last time, Shaun, I would never cheat on you. So if you believe me and trust me, even a bit, stay, I will show you proof, but if you left now, believe me, this is over. I would never forgive you," and I took off the ring he had given me and offered it to him with one hand and held out my phone to show him proof in another. "Choice is yours," I spoke as I closed my eyes.

I felt the ring getting plucked out of my fingers and then a few seconds later, the door was slammed shut. I fell on the floor, howling.

"But I am telling the truth," I sobbed. "I am telling the truth. I would never cheat on you! NEVER!"

Chapter 14

After crying my eyes out, somehow I found my strength to get up. I got dressed, picked up my purse and started to walk out. My heart felt like it was broken in two, and there was no way to measure the pain I was facing in the rest of my body as that man had – he had.... If only Shaun had bothered to ask, he would have known what that man did to me... but he didn't... he just....

Tears still falling, I limped out of the door and found Sam standing there. I was shocked to see him there. All his security was standing in the corridor, and there he was, sitting on the floor like a broken man, with his head in his hands, sobbing hard, right outside the door.

I wanted to sit beside him but his words rang in my ears, *'You cheated on Daksh with me, now you are cheating on me with this pig! You could not wait for me? You could not control yourself!'*

Feeling he had slapped me squarely in the face, I staggered away, with my head held as high as possible.

"Sir," Sam called but I didn't turn to see what was happening. I called the elevator and waited. As the elevator doors opened, I saw him standing right beside me in the mirror of the elevator. I stepped in, he followed and so did his security.

The doors opened, I limped outside, surrounded by his security, but I didn't go to the car in which I had come in. I started walking to the bus stop that I could see across the main road, but he grabbed my hand and pushed me rather rudely in the car. Closing the door in my face, he sat from the other side and we drove home.

All the way nobody said a word. There was a stabbing pain in my stomach but I didn't wince or make any move. He didn't care for my pains and I didn't care to share them with him. A part of me wanted to tell him everything but was it worth it? Whoever planned this had succeeded. Whoever wanted to break us up must be rejoicing now.

We reached home, where I dragged myself to the room to pack my things. Shaun went straight to the bar. Fortunately, this time I had my passport with me. As I opened the wardrobe, I saw three wedding gowns hanging there. I loved all three of them and I was planning to get one finalized when Simi would have arrived in two days' time. But now, what was the use! I hugged the wedding gowns and fell to the ground sobbing. How did my almost wedding turned into this devastation?

Knock! Knock! Knock!

I didn't bother answering but someone entered still.

"I am sorry to enter your room like this." I looked up with foggy eyes, it was Daniel. "But I think there is some grave misunderstanding here."

I didn't reply to this, instead I just placed the wedding gowns on the bed and stared at them.

"For your wedding?" Daniel asked, surprised.

I nodded. "I was planning it on the next weekend. My family is flying in day after," I choked. "I wanted to surprise him when he came back from Brazil. But..."

"He brought me from Brazil because he was planning to marry you next weekend," Daniel supplied. "He was going to surprise you as well. He asked your parents to come down this week. And he even got a visa fast-tracked for your best friend in India."

I blinked back my tears as I stared at Daniel.

"Babi—" Daniel started.

"What?" I was confused.

"Isn't that what you call brother's wife in India? Barbie?" Daniel asked apologetically.

Despite myself, I smiled at his words, "*Bhabhi,*" I corrected him. "Although, this word doesn't hold any value now. I am no one's *bhabhi* now."

"Why don't you tell me exactly what happened," Daniel suggested.

I just shook my head and continued to pack up my things.

"I know what he said and did was harsh, but I would have killed my girlfriend if I saw her semi-naked photos with a stranger," Daniel reasoned.

"Photos?" I blanched.

"Yes," he sighed.

♥

Almost two hours ago –
Somewhere outside London Heathrow Airport

"Oh man, I cannot wait to meet your girl," Daniel spoke as he sat in the car with Shaun and Mia. "I mean I am supposed to be best-man at your wedding, I should at least approve of the girl."

Shaun laughed loudly and Mia growled.

"You don't approve of her?" Daniel asked Mia.

"Well, I don't disapprove of her," Mia rolled her eyes.

"There is nothing to judge okay," Shaun punched Daniel. "She is my life and I am marrying her, sooner than she is anticipating."

"That's why I am here, aren't I?" Daniel laughed.

Beep!

"Ooh, message from the missus!" Daniel teased.

Laughing heartily, Shaun opened the message and saw it was an MMS. Kaya, in nude lingerie, in a hotel room.

Shaun quickly dialled her number, but it was not reachable.

Next message also had an image with Kaya trying on a pair of kinky handcuffs.

Shaun called her security head. "Where is she?" he demanded.

"Hotel Marriot," the security head informed.

"Drive to Hotel Marriott as fast as you can," Shaun barked to the driver.

"What is happening?" Mia asked as she snatched his phone and checked the messages. Shaun had no strength to stop her. *What was Kaya doing in a hotel room in that kind of lingerie?*

"Holy shit! What is she doing?" Mia shrieked.

"What happened?" Daniel took the phone and at the same time another message came. He opened it and stared.

"How far are we from Marriott?" Daniel asked the driver.

"Stopping outside now," the driver informed.

Shaun took back the phone and saw the latest photograph with Kaya pinned against a wall, kissing another man. Blood curdled in his veins as he hopped out of the car and ran upstairs with Mia and Daniel, his security and Kaya's security following him.

♥

Present time in Kaya's and Shaun's bedroom.

"Imagine what he went through," Daniel spoke as he rubbed his face. Kaya couldn't believe it. If Shaun was at the airport, then who did that?

"Also," Daniel continued, "the pact you guys made. Trust even if you found the other in someone else's bed, that's very weird pact to make, isn't it?" Daniel wondered.

"The pact is broken though, isn't it?" I sniffed.

"Would you tell me?" Daniel insisted.

"Why?" I demanded. Everyone here had ulterior motives, I wondered what Daniel wanted.

"Believe me when I say this, I am the only person who is currently willing to sort out your issues. I don't want Shaun's money and I don't want his name, reputation or sister for that matter. I am the only person you can trust, believe me," Daniel insisted.

I looked at him curiously, so he added, "Oh, you don't know, isn't it? Shaun is the owner of world's biggest FMCG brands, and I am the owner of world's biggest alcohol brands. I have less products than Shaun but given our category, we sell massively. Plus margins are super amazing," he laughed proudly.

I just stared at him dumbfounded.

"Look, he is drinking his ass off downstairs. You are packing to leave him permanently up here. I am the only one trying to sort out the misunderstanding between you two. So please tell me everything."

Throwing the shirt I was shoving in my bag on the bed unceremoniously, I slumped to the floor and cried.

He heaved a sigh and sat on the bed and waited.

"Shaun installed WhatsApp," I started.

"Shaun doesn't believe in WhatsApp," Daniel corrected me.

"It was a secret between him and me. His Text messaging broke so he had to converse with me via WhatsApp," I informed.

"Umm… no," and Daniel showed me his phone where Shaun had texted him that morning.

"Here," and I handed my phone to Daniel to show him Shaun's text messages.

Daniel was utterly confused.

"Okay, this is weird," Daniel spoke thoughtfully. "And where does the pact come in?"

And I told him about the wrong number and the girl answering that number!

"And Shaun let that incident slide?" Daniel shook his head in disbelief. I just shrugged.

"Come, let's go and face him," Daniel offered me his hand. "The only person who can really confirm if he is using WhatsApp is Shaun himself. So let's talk to him before he poisons himself with alcohol."

Feeling partially hopeless and partially hopeful, I took his hand and got up. I winced as a stabbing pain shot up in the area around my waist. I cried in pain.

"You are bleeding," he exclaimed and pointed at my legs. And sure enough, I saw a dark line of blood flow down my legs.

In a normal scenario, I would have felt embarrassed for bleeding in front of a stranger like this, but today, I just turned and went to the bathroom to take out my sanitary napkins. I wanted to get rid of the dirty lingerie, but owing to the all the pain in my body, I had no strength to take it off, which I knew would be a fight in itself.

I just wore a panty on top and putting on my pad, I cleaned my legs and stepped out.

"Was he really raping you?" Daniel asked with panicked concern as he saw me step out. I almost fell, feeling dizzy and he supported me. With him still holding my arm to ensure I would not fall, I gobbled a pain killer with some water and nodded in tears.

"What did he do to you?" he asked, panic racing on his face.

I just shook my head as I gripped his shirt for some support. More tears fell down my cheeks at his words.

His grip tightened slightly on my hand as he saw me cry, "We will take care of that pervert bastard too."

Daniel helped me climb down the stairs and made me wait in the drawing room. He then left and dragged in Shaun too, Mia following at his heels.

"What is she doing here?" Mia demanded. I saw Mia was wearing my engagement ring.

Shaun slumped in the sofa next to me and sat with his head hung low.

"Dude, are you on WhatsApp?" Daniel asked.

Shaun snorted.

"And are you conversing with Kaya on WhatsApp?" Daniel added.

Shaun looked up in shock. "I don't even have WhatsApp on my phone!"

"But someone is chatting with her using your number via WhatsApp," Daniel informed and showed him my phone. "I checked the number, it is yours. Someone has tapped into your phone, dude!"

Shaun snatched the phone and looked at it himself.

"May I check your phone?" Daniel asked Shaun.

Shaun unlocked his phone and gave it to him. Daniel then took my phone and compared the messages. "See, it is weird," Daniel spoke. "The messages are exactly the same, it's just that someone is text blocking you on her phone and then passing on your texts to her on WhatsApp!"

"What? Give me that?" Mia intervened and checked for herself.

"Surprise!" Mia read. "WhatsApp chat was a surprise? How stupid are you to believe this crap?" she asked me.

"I asked him, I confirmed with him. And he said even walls have ears so I should shush!" I informed.

"What?" Shaun spoke.

"Remember when you were in South Africa, and you said you have a surprise for me," I reminded him.

"Yeah!" Shaun spoke thoughtfully.

"Wasn't texts on WhatsApp that surprise?" I asked, confused.

"Nooo," Shaun shook his head.

"Then why did you say even walls have ears, I should keep it quiet. Because that's what you wrote in message too," I pointed at my phone, which was still in Mia's hands.

"I didn't write that in message," Shaun looked confused.

"Yep, he didn't write it, but she did receive it," Mia displayed both phones together.

"What did you send then?" Daniel asked, perplexed.

Shaun pressed his lips at this.

"Yeah, what did you send? Because I didn't receive a thing. And you had asked me if I will use it, and I had said yes, daily!" I recalled.

"I had sent –" he paused as he looked at Daniel and Mia.

"Oh, come now, we want to know. We are in smack middle of this tragedy," Mia retorted.

"What?" I asked seriously.

"As I travel a lot, I sent you a *vibrator*," he paused with a mischievous grin, "With a note saying you can use it when you are alone and if you are comfortable when you are with me too..."

Mia and Daniel snickered, I turned red.

"Why would I need a – a—*that*," I shouted.

"Well, I never saw you use it with me but you were so happy when I sent it, so I thought you just want to use it when I am not there," Shaun shrugged.

"Because... ah right!" I spoke sarcastically, "I could not wait for a week, isn't it? I have to have a fuck! Right?"

"See, wait," Daniel interjected.

"In all fairness, he didn't know anything. He got messages with your, well photos, and he just lost it. Anybody would. And, Shaun, dude, seriously she was set up. That bastard was really raping her," Daniel finished.

Shaun's face turned blank for a moment, as if a million thoughts were racing in his mind. He then got up and fell on his knees. Placing his head on my thighs, he cried so heavily that along with him, my entire body shook.

"I am sorry," he spoke between his sobs. "I am so sorry."

"Err... I hate to intervene at this moment but, Shauny, do you believe your girl is not cheating on you," Daniel asked to confirm.

Shaun nodded in my thighs.

"*Bhbhai,*" he spoke.

"*Bhaaaabhiii,*" I corrected him.

"Oh yes, Bhabhi, you forgive Shaun for almost hitting you, shoving you, calling you names and all the shit?" he asked.

A part of me didn't want to forgive Shaun, but another part, that loved him incredibly and knew he was not at fault, forgave him. I nodded too.

"Cool, so wedding is back on. And guessing you have 3 wedding gowns to choose from, I am going to select one and send back the other two, okay?" Daniel laughed.

I nodded and Shaun looked up, shocked.

"Oh yes, she too planned to marry you next weekend. Oh, you guys are just a match made in heaven," Daniel laughed heartily.

"Here," Mia gave us our phones back with a disappointed look.

"Geez, don't look so glum, Mia," Daniel mocked, "If you will act like this, these guys will have a reason to believe that you are the mastermind behind this plan to separate them."

"I could not, even if tried to, this all started when he was in South Africa, so—" Mia growled.

"South Africa, Ron was there with me," Shaun spoke out loud.

"Ron holds a grudge against Kaya, believe me," Mia informed. "She stabbed herself when you were supposed to be in Australia to save Ron's ass from that court case. He had to pay the penalty out of his own pocket as it was his mistake that we landed in that trouble, and you were practically unavailable for days at that time."

"Which one is Ron?" Daniel asked.

"Oh, the worst of our cousins. He got into so much trouble here that he was shipped off to Australia," Mia scoffed.

"What kind of trouble?" Daniel asked seriously and he took my phone from me and typed something on it.

"Oh, you name it," Mia supplied, "Drugs, fights, hacking, gaming, you name it."

"Hacking?" Daniel asked, stunned. "Shaun, what message did you just get?"

"I am sorry, please forgive me, from Kaya," Shaun read with bloodshot eyes.

"One second," and Mia took Shaun's phone and typed something. "What reply did you get?" she asked as my phone chimed a minute later.

"I hate you, stay away from me!" Daniel read out loud. "Oh, come on, Mia!" he scolded.

Mia showed Daniel the phone she was holding.

"Ingenious," Daniel muttered.

"So, Mia sent the message from Shaun's phone, *I love you and I forgive you.* And Kaya got the message *I hate you, stay away from me!*" Daniel read.

Shaun jumped to his heels and read the messages himself.

"This needs expert hacking," Daniel added. "And your phones are cloned, for sure. Want my IT team to look into it?" he offered.

Shaun nodded, lost in his thoughts. I was sure he was not aware what he was agreeing to.

"Have you met this Ron?" Daniel asked me.

I shook my head.

"Then who cloned your phone?" Daniel wondered. "Someone would need to access your phone, especially, for that incident where someone changed the number."

"I don't leave my phone alone in office at any time," I informed, "you know, as I don't want to miss a message or call from him," I pointed at Shaun.

Shaun looked at me for a second and was about to say something when I added, "But at home, most of the time I am unable to find my phone as I don't care where I throw it, especially, if he is with me!"

Shaun again opened his mouth to speak something but Daniel interrupted him, "When did you notice the number was changed?"

"It's weird actually and I told him as well. I had called him the previous day and it was fine but the next day his number was different, which I understood only when he pointed it out. I was just looking at his name," I shrugged.

"I—" Shaun started but Daniel interrupted again, "You have cameras in this house? Isn't it?"

"Yes," I nodded, "everywhere except the rooms."

"Hmm… we need to check footage of your office and home around that day," Daniel suggested.

"I already got every second of the day checked for office to see who touched her phone. No one did," Shaun added hastily.

"You did? I thought you said it was some practical joke?" I asked, shocked.

"Of course, I said that, but it doesn't mean I won't check who did it," Shaun looked exasperated.

"So now we check your house. We also need to see who swiped that 'surprise package' that your Romeo sent you,"

Daniel snickered and I felt my face burn again. "But we have to be careful, it can be anyone. How many people work in this house?"

"Around twenty, and I am going to fire every single one of them," Shaun barked.

"What? No, you cannot do that," I expressed my shock.

"Someone in the house betrayed us. Put you at risk!" Shaun snapped.

"And they will be punished, but not the innocent, okay," I stressed.

"So who has access to all the recordings?" Daniel asked.

"Sam has access to everything," Shaun shrugged.

"I will talk to your giant," Daniel agreed.

"Can I speak with you? In private?" Shaun asked me.

"Yeah, I will head to my room, I am hoping my usual room is available for me to occupy?" Daniel asked Shaun and I.

Shaun nodded and informed me that Daniel always stayed in the downstairs guest room with Shaun whenever he came from Brazil.

"I have no room here, so I will take your leave then," Mia shrugged. "It is – well –" she paused to look at me, "I am pleased to know you are not cheating on my brother because believe me, if you did, you would have been dead by now!" and after giving me a very uncomfortable, very awkward hug, she moved out.

"Oh, I think that's hers," Daniel pointed at my engagement ring.

Mia rolled her eyes and dropped it on the side table and left.

Daniel passed the ring to Shaun and said "Adios, love birds..."

Shaun nodded as he looked at me.

"And I know this is the last thing either of you want, but make a scene, Shaun, shout at her, insult her so whoever is keeping a tab on you guys inside your house will pass on the info to Ron or whoever is after you. Then, she can rush after you, you can make a lot of noise in the room, like you are fighting and not sex noises, and then you can leave or stay, whatever you wish to do, okay?"

Shaun nodded again, squeezing my hand.

Daniel gave one last look of pity and left.

Shaun kissed my hand and whispered, "Sorry for this..." and then he too followed Daniel out shouting, "I cannot believe you betrayed me like this. It is absolutely unacceptable. Stay away from me."

And though I knew he was pretending, though I knew he didn't mean it, I couldn't help but feel my heart sink. I sat down and tried to relax but couldn't. I tried to breathe calmly but could not.

A part of me was glad Shaun didn't ask me what that man did to me, but another part of me, the one that needed comfort to get rid of the trauma I had endured today, desperately wanted him to.

I looked around the massive drawing room. I was all alone. Feeling broken and hopeless, I just sank to the floor and sobbed.

I don't know for how long I cried there, but by the time I heard someone enter the room, I was howling with pain.

"Hey," it was Daniel who had come back, looking for me. "Hey... hey... shhh," he patted my head to comfort me, but there was no comfort he could offer me. I didn't know what was happening and I had never felt this bad in my entire life.

"Kaya, please," he spoke and tried to lift my head, but I couldn't. I just couldn't find it in me to stop crying.

"Hey, come here..." and he forced me up and hugged me tightly. Hugging him back, I sobbed in his chest. So loudly that I couldn't hear what he was saying.

He moved and spoke something but I didn't know what. A few minutes later, I felt someone thud beside me.

"No... no... I am sorry... please, I am sorry," it was Shaun and Daniel passed my sobbing self to his arms.

"You didn't come," I cried, "I called you, when he was – when he was – I begged you to come. But you didn't come... why didn't you come? You didn't believe me, why didn't you believe me?" and I cried again in his arms.

"I will never forgive myself for it," he whispered in my ears.

"You didn't come," I cried again as I clutched his collar and shook him. He didn't fight and let me hit him on his chest. "You didn't... you didn't..." I shouted.

"I don't want this," I pushed him after a while and looked at him. He was tear stricken and devastated. "I don't want you and your life. I was happier when I was in India. My mother was right. I never listened to her. You will be the end of me, and look where I am standing right now. Everyone, including you, calling me a whore, I don't want this. I am leaving," and with one push at his chest, I stood up and walked upstairs.

I didn't know whether he was following me or not, but I didn't care. I rushed to my room and looked for my passport, but it was not on the bed where I had kept it. I tossed and turned everything but it was not there, and neither were my wedding dresses.

"Looking for this?" he asked. He was standing by the door, with my passport in his hands. As I knew he wouldn't give it to me, I didn't even attempt to take it from him.

I wanted to go out but I knew he would not let me get out of the room as well. So I moved to the bathroom, however before I could lock it, he was there too.

"Please, listen," he begged. I just shook my head. "Let's get you cleaned up first, where does it hurt?" he asked seriously.

"Please, go," I whispered.

"I won't make that mistake again," he replied, pushing me in the shower and turning it on. As hot water rushed all over me, I realized how filthy I felt.

He undid my dress and dropped it from my soaking body.

"We should burn this," he whispered as he looked at the lingerie I was still wearing. "You should have known I would never ask you to wear this. This is so not my taste."

I shot him a dirty look and he apologized again. He hopped out of the shower and brought back a pair of scissors. Slowly, carefully, he cut the dress and I was free, finally. The bands of the dress had dug into my skin, leaving marks.

"It was one size too tight," he whispered as he bent to kiss my shoulder where there was a mark of the dress digging in, but I moved away.

"I apologize, again," he sighed, grabbing my waist and pulling me close to him. I winced as his hand moved on my stomach. He tried to make me turn but I didn't let him. I looked down at my waist and a big, reddish-blue patch was appearing on my lower abdomen. I covered it with my hands, shielding it from him.

"I apologize over and over. I am sorry. Truly. Deeply. Sincerely."

I took a quick shower, while he stood with me fully dressed, then putting on the first nightwear I could lay my hands upon, I slipped into bed. He too changed and slipped in with me, hugging me tightly from behind.

"At least look at me," he begged; I didn't reply. "Or shout at me, please."

I didn't reply again.

"Say something," he pleaded. But hearing my silence, he grabbed my hand and hit his face with full force.

I sat bolt upright at this, glaring at him. I was appalled by his behaviour. "Hit me," he requested. But I just climbed out of the bed and went to the wardrobe to dress properly to step out.

I took off the nighty I was wearing and put on a jeans and a t-shirt and turned to step out, only to find him on his knees, in the middle of the room, with his head hung low. My anger melted as I saw him like this.

He raised my passport in his hand and spoke with his head still bowed, "I know you want this. You can have it. You are not here as a prisoner; you are here as my partner and I won't force you to stay with me."

I took the passport and pocketed it. My anger was lightening slightly, but I needed space, so I started to leave, when he spoke, "Will you at least listen to me, please? A few minutes is all I ask," he begged.

I stood by the door and waited. He didn't move, just sat there as if in punishment and spoke, "I know I hurt you and all this is my fault. You came here for me. You have no friends here. You have no family. You have me, and only me. And yet, it is twice in just a matter of few months when I have done something incredibly wrong. When I have hurt you to the point of no return. I have hit you in the head, I have avoided you for fifteen days, I have shouted at you, I have called you names, I have even now hurt you," he inhaled heavily. "But you have only loved me unconditionally. Because of me you became a target today. You were almost raped. And I was not there. I know I have wronged you on many levels. You are trying your best to bear with me, adjust in my world, but all I have given you is a hard time, and I am sorry for it."

I sat on the floor by the door at these words. Partially he was right, but I knew he too loved me just as much as I loved him.

"You want to go back, I get it," he sighed. "We all want to escape to people we love when we are threatened. And today, I have endangered you, so it is natural you wish to go back home.

And I won't stop you. You can go, I will drop you to the airport myself, but please, *please, please, please* promise me that you will come back to me. That when the dust settles, when you are calm, you will return to me. Please promise me as much and I won't follow you to heaven and hell."

No reply again. I had no words to say to him.

"I will give up everything," he continued, "Money, power, my position as CEO, everything for you. Just come back to me, okay," he begged.

I stood up and wanted to run to him, but something in me stopped me, maybe that part of my ego which had got hurt by his comment on cheating on Daksh and him. I opened the door to go and he drew a huge breath of cry. I wanted to leave, but another part of me, which loved him unconditionally, didn't let me. And the part which was thankful that despite everything he had stayed back, had waited for me outside that hotel room won. Quietly I closed the door and sat on the bed, staring at his broken form.

He was sobbing now, crying just as harshly as I had cried. He fell on all fours and curled up on the floor and cried. And this was too much for me.

"Shaun!" I whispered.

He paused for a moment, then cried again.

"Where could I ever go without you?" I asked. He got up immediately and looked up, tears racing down his face.

"You are here!" he whispered.

"Heaven may fall or Hell may rise, no matter what happens in this world, I will never leave your side," I smiled.

Despite his swollen face, his eyebrows arched, "I didn't know you write proses and poetries," he smiled.

"Neither did I," I shrugged as I stood up again. "I want some space today."

"You went through terrible ordeal today, you need me," he insisted.

"Maybe, maybe not," I replied.

At this, he got up and sat on the sofa that was placed in our room. "I will sleep on the sofa tonight, okay?"

"No," I shrieked.

"You have your space, but you will stay in front of my eyes. And if you feel sick, scared or anything negative, I will be there with you," he stressed. "Okay?"

I nodded.

He got up and brought his pillow to the sofa.

"Just one thing though," he spoke as I changed back into my nightwear.

"What?" I asked, sitting in bed.

"Two actually," he smiled.

"What?" I asked.

"One hug and one kiss, please," he requested.

I looked at him gravely, then nodded. He walked up to me, and pressed his lips firmly on mine. I felt pain ease from every inch of my body as he kissed me deeply. And then after a while, he wrapped his hands around my body and squeezed me so tightly that it seemed he would push me inside him.

"I am sorry," he whispered again. "So, so sorry for not being there for you when you needed me the most."

"It's okay now," I patted him clumsily.

"Huh!" he breathed loudly and caressed my cheek.

"Now I know the answer to my very old question," I smiled.

"Which question?" he asked seriously.

"Remember when on Marine Drive," I started and his face hardened, "remember I asked you what would you do if I were your wife and you saw a picture of me kissing another man!"

"You want me to kill myself?" he asked in devastated tone.

"You and I are linked, killing one is killing another and I want to live a very long, happy and rich life. So stay alive, okay," I ordered.

"Your wish is my command," he whispered, smiling.

"You didn't receive this message, isn't it? When I first wrote to you 'your wish is always my command?'" I asked seriously.

He shook his head and his smile disappeared.

"Good night, my love," he pushed back my hair and kissed my forehead. "Tomorrow, I need to find the culprit behind all our miseries."

I nodded as he went back to the sofa. "And thank you," he added.

"For what?" I asked as I closed my eyes.

"For giving me, *us,* another chance."

Chapter 15

I woke with a start, drenched in sweat and saw my bed empty. I looked at the sofa and Shaun was not there too.

Heart racing, I started to get out of bed and found him sitting on the floor, beside me, with his head on the side of the bed.

I stared at him for a second, he was holding a fistful of my clothes tightly. Calming my nerves a bit, I caressed his face. He woke up with a start.

"What? Are you okay?" he asked suddenly.

"What are you doing here?" I whispered.

"You were getting restless in your sleep, I should have brought in a counsellor last night to talk to you," he rubbed his eyes.

"But you are on the floor," I pointed. "Why?"

"Space," he shrugged and I felt guilty. I shifted and made space for him and pulled him in my arms.

"I am fine here," he spoke, sitting back on the floor.

"I don't need space, I need you, only you," I replied sombrely. "I don't think I ever want anything or anyone else when I have you around me."

A smile, filled with genuine relief, etched on his face as he climbed in the bed beside me.

"I am sorry, once again," he repeated. "Though I dread to ask, what did that man do to you?" he asked in a frightful tone.

"Let it be, it is okay now," I patted his head affectionately.

"It is not. What I said, what I did," he spoke sadly.

"Let's make one more deal this time," I spoke before he repeated his yesterday's actions.

"I like your deals. It is because of that deal I waited outside the room. I was angry and furious and hurt, but deep down I knew you would not betray me," he kissed my forehead.

"And yet you almost hit me!" I asked, confused.

At this he climbed on top of me and spoke, "It was a wrong reaction, I am way too sorry," he pressed his face in my shoulder and continued muttering 'sorry'.

"Okay, another deal," I continued and he looked in my eyes curiously.

"We will make mistakes, we will hurt each other," I started. He was about to say something but I placed my hand on his mouth and continued, "This is how relationships work. We cannot live without disappointing each other, hurting each other, or fighting with each other. But you have to promise me that no matter what happens, we will not lose trust in each other. We will always trust." He nodded.

"...and we will always forgive the other one for their action and ourself for our reaction."

His eyes lit up at these words.

"And," I continued, "if the other person is genuinely sorry, I mean 'genuinely' and not sarcastically or just for the sake of saying, we have to let go of our anger within twenty-four hours."

He nodded again.

"Cool, so stop apologizing, okay!" I stressed.

"Fine," he sighed and rolled to his side of the bed. "But..." he hesitated, "did he hurt you? That bastard?"

I looked at him for a second, then decided to lie, "I am fine."

He nodded, grabbed my hand and kissed it, "I am truly sorry again."

"Oh, enough with your sorries," I shouted.

"Fine," he grumbled and lay straight.

"Out of all your friends, I like Daniel the most," I spoke after a pause. "He is sensible one. He really supported me yesterday."

"Yeah, he is the best," Shaun smiled.

"Where are my wedding gowns, by the way?" I asked.

"He took them saying it is bad luck for me to see any option of the wedding gown before the actual wedding," he laughed at these words. "Good thing he came, how else I would have known you were downstairs, crying!"

I looked at him sadly, so he added, "When you didn't follow us, he decided to go check, then he called me while you were crying."

"God, I was such a mess," I exclaimed, embarrassed.

"Well, to be honest, neither of us are good at dealing with tears, and well, yours were a storm," he laughed. And when I glared at him, he added, "For good reason though. Reasons for which I am not going to apologize anymore, but yes, fair enough reasons."

I shook my head in exasperation.

"So are you ready to get married next weekend?" he asked happily.

"I am reconsidering," I sighed.

"What?" he sat up straight. "Why?"

"With everything that's going on!" I added.

"It doesn't matter. We are getting married. And if you will try to postpone, we will get married tomorrow," he threatened.

I stared at him with mixed expressions, how should I tell him why I wanted to postpone.

"Can I tell you by evening?" I requested.

"Why? What's happening during the day?" he narrowed his eyes.

I rubbed my stomach and looked away. "Nothing is happening, I just need some space!"

He knew I was lying so he glared at me.

"You are lying," he accused.

"Evening," I repeated and got out of bed to get freshened up.

"Where are you going?" he asked seriously.

"It's morning now. I need to find out who the heck is trying so hard to disrupt our life and happiness and for that we have plenty of work to do."

Chapter 16

Things moved very quickly in the morning. Daniel and Sam – the head of security – scanned through the video recordings of the house and found the culprit. It was one of the handmaids Sarina had hired under her to cater to my needs, her name was Maria.

Shaun was beside himself when he saw footages of Maria take away the parcel and sneak into our room at odd hours.

"Why is she able to access your room so easily? Weren't you in there?" Daniel asked as he showed me a video footage.

"I think doc gave me sleeping pills so they knocked me out pretty bad," I informed.

"The doctor didn't give you sleeping pills," Shaun intervened. "I had asked him about every single medicine he prescribed to you, and though one had some sedative effect, none was a sleeping pill!"

I was stunned by this.

"Well, I don't know, one out of the six must be sleeping pill," I informed.

"Five," Shaun corrected.

"Six, I was taking them, I remember taking six pills each night," I corrected him and Shaun looked appalled.

"Maybe that's why you were always asleep when I left or came home!" Shaun wondered. "I used to get so angry that you didn't care to wait for me!"

I looked at him in surprise, "And I thought you were avoiding me because you came in after I fell asleep and left before I woke up."

"For two people who love each other so much," Daniel commented, "you both need to interact more."

"Oh, we interact, okay!" Shaun retorted.

"Yeah, not just with your bodies and mouths, but also with words," he teased and Shaun mock punched him.

"Where is this Maria?" Daniel asked.

"She must be in the house, I saw her this morning," I informed.

"Where?" Shaun asked.

"She came to our room to collect something from the bedside, remember," I reminded him.

"I don't even look at their faces," Shaun shrugged.

"Well, I know and remember faces of everyone who works in our house," I looked at him in disbelief.

"And in office?" Shaun asked impressed.

"Office too," I shrugged. "I know and talk to everyone starting from door man to cleaner."

"Wow!" Daniel looked impressed too.

"There is no wow factor here. You people may have a line of 'rich' and 'poor' in your heads, but to me, we all are same," I looked shocked at their reactions.

"That's why I love you so much," Shaun bent to kiss me but I pushed him.

"Why don't you talk to Maria, and I will go and wrap up some things," I spoke.

"Where are you going?" Shaun asked seriously.

"To have another affair," I spoke with narrowed eyes and Shaun growled at my back.

As I walked out, Daniel chased after me.

"I assume you are going to the doctor," he spoke quietly.

"How?" I was shocked.

"The way you bled yesterday, I guessed as much. And I know you are putting up a brave face to save his feelings, isn't it? Your stomach is hurting?" he asked as he stared at my tummy. "Why is your stomach hurting so much? Did that bastard—?"

He left the question hanging and I didn't reply as well.

"What did he do?" Daniel asked, worried and angry.

"Keep Shaun occupied, okay?" I requested.

"Which doctor are you going to, just in case," Daniel asked.

"Nadine booked an appointment for me this morning," I informed as I sat in the car. "David knows the address, I don't! Keep Shaun busy, okay," I requested again and closed the door. He nodded and waved.

♥

Despite getting super preferential treatment at the doctor's, it took me four hours to wrap up the appointment. Well, the first fifteen minutes were spent with me sitting in the doctor's cabin while David and two other security men swept the place for potential listening devices and other threats. I assumed after yesterday's incidence, they were super-extra vigilant.

If David and other were thorough, they were nothing in comparison to how thorough the doctor was. She needed to know everything that had happened yesterday. Tears leaked my eyes as I repeated what that bastard did to me and while she consoled me, she also prescribed therapy.

She ran a few tests, did ultrasounds of various body parts and then after discussing everything thoroughly, she concluded the diagnosis and allowed me leave after prescribing handful of medicines and vitamins I needed for the pain to stop.

"Mr Malani sir has called every fifteen minutes for the past two hours, ma'am," David informed me when I sat back in the car. "He has also asked me to take away your phone as it is dangerous," and he extended his hand for me to give it to him.

I handed him my phone quietly.

"He must be worried sick," I spoke after a while.

"After yesterday's events, I am surprised I am still driving you," David replied. "I thought Mr Malani would have me killed, but he didn't!"

"What? Why?" I asked, shocked.

"I should have accompanied you to the room, ensured you were safe," David explained and he looked sideways at the other man who was sitting next to him.

"You are new?" I asked the other man. He nodded.

"Previous one got fired for not protecting you yesterday," David informed.

"He did what I asked him to," I started.

"It doesn't matter," the other man spoke flatly. "What you ask is irrelevant when it comes to your protection. You cannot be left unguarded at any cost," he added.

David, who had been driving me since day one, spoke, "It doesn't matter, ma'am. It's done. And Sam sir is way too strict. I am here because technically I am not supposed to follow you inside a premises, though now I have been asked to do the same as well."

Feeling bad for the old security guy, I sat back quietly.

"What do you mean by unguarded at any cost?" I asked as he entered the premises of Airia.

The man hopped out of the car and opened the door for me before I could, "We are your shadow, ma'am. You don't need to know where we are. You just need to know, we are there."

And feeling exceptionally pissed, I walked inside.

Shaun was sitting on the stairs outside, waiting for me.

"David told you I am arriving or are you sitting here since morning?" I asked as I walked up to him with a smile. Was I imagining it or was he looking more downtrodden than this morning?

"File?" he asked without another word.

"I don't–" I started but he snatched the huge folder from my hand and led the way inside.

Daniel was sitting inside, working on his laptop. He too looked exceptionally grim.

"Who died?" I asked the duo but they both didn't reply. They didn't even look at me. "Is the word about yesterday's event out in the media?" I gasped.

They didn't reply again so I looked for my phone, but of course, it was with David. Slowly I walked to Daniel, and without asking took his laptop and tried to open the web browser.

"No, it has not leaked, yet!" Daniel replied curtly.

"Hey, what happened to you?" I asked him, shocked.

He was about to say something but taking one look at Shaun and he left.

"Your reports are clean?" Shaun asked as he read through every single page of my folder.

"Yes, just need some medication and rest," I replied unsure about what to tell him.

"And therapy," Shaun added as he read through. "What did you overwrite here?" he asked pointing at a line which I had smudged on so he could not read it.

"Doctor made some mistake," I lied.

He closed his eyes in anger.

"I am fine, truly," I started but Shaun looked so sharply at me that I winced.

"Did you find anything useful from Maria?" I asked seriously.

"Yes," Shaun sighed, "she had added sleeping pills to your medication. She even drugged you so you would feel lethargic all day. And she was getting paid by Ron, as Mia had suspected."

"Okay," I sighed in relief. "So this is over?"

"Yes, Ron and Maria won't bother us anymore. Ron had our phones cloned so they are getting replaced as we speak. Security is also working to ensure there is no other surveillance on us," Shaun added flatly.

"Okay," I replied.

"Okay," he added.

"You are upset with me," I asked, "Why?"

He just shook his head and huffed, "I will take you upstairs, then I have to go for some work."

"What work? I thought you had cancelled everything today," I narrowed my eyes.

"Let's get you upstairs," he spoke as he dragged me to our room.

"What are you hiding?" he asked as he placed me on the bed and handed me my laptop, TV remote and a novel I was planning to read. "Laptop is clean," he added. "You should rest and not move," he explained as I stared at his generous hospitality.

"Thank you," I replied. He noticed that I was clutching my purse very tightly.

Knock! Knock! Knock!

Shaun opened the door and Daniel spoke, "They are ready for us."

"Who is ready for you?" I asked. His tone was severe, it felt like they were going to murder someone.

"Shaun?" I asked seriously. "Where are you going?" I demanded.

He looked at me and then left without a word.

I got out of the bed and ran after him, but sudden shooting pains in my stomach didn't allow me. I was by the stairs when I fell on my knees, crying. I would have tumbled down two flights of stairs if someone had not grabbed me from behind. I saw Shaun rush back upstairs, but before he could reach me, I passed out.

Chapter 17

A few hours ago – In Airia

"You know where she is going?" Shaun demanded from Daniel.

"It is her business," Daniel raised his hand and shrugged. Shaun looked angry but he had other important things.

"I think they are ready for us," Daniel spoke as he read a message on his phone.

Both Shaun and Daniel went to Shaun's home office and connected to a video call.

"Shauny!" Ron's cheerful voice came from the screen. Shaun fisted his fingers to control his rage. "Mind telling me why am I being deported suddenly?"

"I know what you did," Shaun spoke through gritted teeth.

A concern flashed on Ron's face and he looked around. He was on a plane back to London and had nowhere to hide.

"What did I do?" Ron asked carelessly.

"I have Maria," Shaun spoke in a threatening tone. "I know what you did! I mean how could you? Do you have any idea what you put Kaya through? And for what?"

"Oh, I have all the ideas," Ron grinned like a maniac. "Did your princess tell you what happened with her?"

"Why?" Daniel demanded. "Why go through all the trouble?"

"Because I want him out of the picture," and Ron pointed at Shaun. "I hate you, man," he spoke.

"What is wrong with him?" Daniel asked quizzically. "This is open hostility."

"He is drugged," Shaun informed with a shrug, "I made my team inject him with drugs that make people susceptible to other people's will, you know!"

Daniel looked impressed, "Didn't know you had it handy."

"It is always handy when it comes to interrogating bastards like him," Shaun spat as he looked at Ron.

"True," Ron spoke as he raised his hand, "I am a bastard."

"Why did you do it?" Shaun asked curtly.

"Because I hate you, Shauny," Ron grinned. "And for the first time in my life I saw you cry for a girl. And I knew she is your Achilles heel. I knew to get to you, I had to get to her. I had been planning it for a while now. I tried to get her in India, but you had her so heavily guarded there, I couldn't dare. Then you brought her to London, to preserve her in your precious house. I planted my mole in your home who gave me regular updates about how you both were living and what your relationship was!"

"So you asked Maria to add wrong number in Kaya's phone under my name and give her sleeping pills," Shaun demanded.

"Maria did many things for me, a few of them were what you said," Ron waved his hand.

"And this plot to have Kaya raped!" Shaun fisted his hand.

"Oh, it worked wonderfully, isn't it? A shame you arrived before it could happen. The man took it as personal insult when she hit him. You should have seen what he did to her!" A cold shiver ran down Shaun's body at these words.

"What did he do to her?" Shaun shouted.

"Ask your team to send the video in my laptop, you will see," and he laughed.

Shaun called the man who was guarding Ron on the plane and demanded to send the video, "And I swear to God if you watched it or leaked it, I will find you and bury your entire family," he threatened his man who was instructed to pass on the video.

"You are dead, you know, Ron," Daniel spoke in a calm but dangerous voice. "For all your actions, you will not live to see tomorrow's sunrise."

"I know," and Ron giggled. "I didn't know they will talk and make up. I assumed as Shauny is, he will take it on his ego and throw that bitch out. But you guys made up..." and he laughed again.

"Video is here," Shaun informed as he rubbed his fingers in panic. It was clear that he was scared to watch what had happened.

"Watch – watch... and consider it as the best revenge from my side. Watch," and waving with a wide grin on his face, Ron logged off.

"I think I should watch it alone," Daniel suggested.

"No," Shaun whispered as he played the video.

The room was in darkness for a while, then Kaya entered. She had the phone in her hands and she looked stunned with what she was seeing.

"Oh my God! Shaun!" she exclaimed as she stared at her phone's screen. She took off her coat and dress, placed them in the closet and checked herself in its mirror. Her expressions were partially confused and partially disgusted.

"What has gotten into you?" she muttered as she tried to put on the handcuffs.

She fiddled with them for a few seconds then threw them on the bed. "Tie me yourself, if you like," she huffed and then she turned off the lights.

Daniel and Shaun stared at each other as for a minute the room was in darkness. Then they heard the door open, and Shaun gripped Daniel's arm in fear. He knew who was entering!

Daniel paused and looked at Shaun with pity, but Shaun just let the video play.

"I have been waiting for you," Kaya's happy musical voice came in the darkness. But as the light flickered on, her expressions turned horrified.

She jumped out of the bed, covering herself with the bedsheet.

"Who are you?" she demanded. The scared look on her face was too much for Shaun to bear, but he watched on.

"For 10 pounds an hour, I could have you all day," the man spoke lecherously as he moved towards her.

"Stop, I mean it stop," she threatened.

"Oh, take 100 pounds for an hour, just be mine, don't wait," he spoke grabbing the sheet she was using to cover herself.

"Get out, you are in the wrong room, just go!" she shouted.

"Oh, I am not going anywhere, darling," and with one tug, he pulled the sheet, leaving her exposed.

"SHAUN!" she shouted. "SHAUN!"

Shaun made sudden movement as if trying to jump inside the screen to save her, protect her, but he was helpless.

"James, that's my name," the man spoke as he pushed her on the wall and kissed her fiercely.

Kaya tried to push him with all her might, but he was too heavily built against her frame. He grabbed her wrists and tucked them on top. His legs were pinning against hers and no matter how hard she tried to wriggle, she couldn't move.

"HELP ME! HELP! HELP!" she shouted but he placed his second hand on her mouth and looked at her with threat.

"I will kill you if you don't let it happen," he barked.

Tears escaped her as he tried to undo his pants. Finding an opening, she raised her knee and gave a hard kick in his groin.

The man howled with pain and rage as he sat on the floor.

She rushed out but the man grabbed her legs and she fell hard on the floor. He stood up, grabbed her hair and kicked her hard in the stomach.

"Quite a bitch you are, aren't you?" he barked.

"Shaun!" she cried, grabbing her stomach and writhing in pain.

Shaun was now on his knees, tears falling non-stop as he saw his Kaya in such situation.

"Who is this Shaun?" the man demanded as he grabbed her and pushed her on the bed. "Are you wearing this," and he grabbed her body in all inappropriate places, "for him?" and he pushed his hand in between her legs and inside her.

A sharp sound of pain escaped her mouth and her mouth hung open in dread and terror as she registered what was happening to her.

The man pulled out his hand and licked it.

"Please, stop!" she begged. "Please…" she cried. "Shaun, where are you?"

"Your Shaun is not here, but I am here," and he undid his pants. He was about to drop it when the door burst open and a few people entered the room.

Daniel paused the screen and looked at Shaun. He too was crying.

"And after she endured all that, I hit her!" Shaun wailed.

"You almost hit her… you stopped…" Daniel corrected.

"I wanted to…" Shaun cried.

"She is at the doctor's," Daniel informed. "She was bleeding last night, so she is at the doctor to get checked up," Daniel finished as he swallowed to wet his dry throat.

"Bleeding?" Shaun asked, worried.

"Can you blame she is bleeding?" Daniel pointed at the screen.

"How could I do that to her? I claim to love her and I –" Shaun cried.

"If I be honest, I am amazed by her love. She truly loves you, she forgave you after everything," Daniel spoke after a thought. "Women amaze me!"

"What should I do?" Shaun asked sadly.

"Few things for starters. Kill this bastard," Daniel pointed at the screen, "and take care of Kaya at all costs, okay."

♥

Present time – in the hospital.

When I came to, I was in the hospital. Shaun was beside me, looking devastated.

"Oh no!" I cried as I registered my surroundings.

"Didn't I ask you to stay in bed?" he asked through gritted teeth.

"You were not talking to me and if I didn't know any better, you looked like you were going to murder someone," I replied.

"Like you are talking to me!" he shouted.

"Fine, go! I don't want to talk to you anymore," I muttered and turned away.

He closed his eyes, fisted his fingers and rushed outside.

"Now what happened?" Daniel came in after a moment.

"You too, get away," I shouted at him too, tears leaking my eyes now.

"I would have asked you to watch your tone but given what happened and the loss you suffered, I am going to give you a free pass for a few days," Daniel spoke grimly.

"My loss?" I asked, thunderstruck.

"We know!" Daniel raised his eyebrows, "I am appalled, imagine his condition."

I closed my eyes in disbelief. Damn that doctor!

"Whom did you murder?" I asked with eyes still closed.

"Yet to murder, your hospitalization took precedence," he spoke, sitting beside my bed.

I stared at him in shock.

"We recovered yesterday's entire video from Ron's hard drive. We, i.e. Shaun and I, saw what that man did to you!" Daniel informed and another set of tears trickled down my cheek.

Suddenly flashes of that horrific event flashed in front of my eyes. Him kicking me in the stomach. Me kicking him in the groin. Him pushing me on the bed. Grabbing my mouth to stop me from screaming. Pushing his hand in me just for vengeance and pleasure.

Just the memory of it sent shooting pains down my body.

"I am terribly sorry for what you had to endure," Daniel continued.

"I was not raped," I whispered.

"Getting fucked is not the only definition of rape, and if it is, it is wrong!" Daniel wiped his forehead. "You endured all that and then you had to suffer Shaun's wrath. I cannot blame you for breaking down yesterday, and I am in awe of you for forgiving him."

"Will you stop him from committing murder?" I asked sadly.

"After knowing that I lost my first God-Child due to that pervert bastard, God no!" Daniel hissed. "This is going to change Shaun, okay," Daniel added, "you need to give him time to cope, okay?"

"What?" I asked, aghast.

"I know you need time too, but --"

"I did not have a miscarriage," I shouted.

"Oh, you didn't even know you were carrying?" Daniel asked morosely.

"No, I was not pregnant," I repeated.

"You bled heavily and the doctor said—" Daniel started, "Are you sure?" he asked, confused.

"Of course, I am sure," I stressed. "I had my periods not even fifteen days ago! Shaun knows it."

"Well, forgive him for not knowing how many days here and there," Daniel shrugged.

"Oh God, no wonder he is so glum," I cried. "Please, let him know."

"I will," Daniel spoke thoughtfully.

"Go find him and tell him NOW!" I stressed.

"Oh right," and Daniel rushed out.

♥

Shaun and Daniel didn't come back for a few hours. However, the doctor came and discussed the situation with me. This was another doctor, so she was not aware of the discussion I had with the one during the morning visit.

"My apologies for miscommunication to Mr Malani," the doctor apologized. "He couldn't tell me your last menstrual date and I just mentioned that severe bleed could be a sign of miscarriage and they assumed the worst."

"Splendid, really!" I scathed.

"Still, just to be sure," she asked, "your last period was on 19th of this month?"

I nodded.

"So that's fourteen days and when was your last intercourse?" she asked.

"25th," I growled.

"Then you cannot be pregnant," she confirmed.

"I know," I shouted. "And I had a blood work done this morning to confirm! Shouldn't you have tested too, before activating the rumour mill?"

"My apologies again," she added. "You bled because your uterus suffered injury yesterday, and along with the injury of your last accident, together it caused some damage to your abdomen."

"Just amazing!" I scowled.

"How did you get that scar?" she pointed at my stomach.

"None of your concern," I snapped.

"Fair enough! You have a right to be annoyed with me. I misdiagnosed you," she added calmly. "But if I may ask, the scar didn't stop bothering you, didn't it?"

"No, it still hurt sometimes," I replied curtly.

"Because it didn't heal correctly," she added. "My treatment will heal you now!"

She left with a smile while I stared after her thinking she was the last person I would ever seek treatment from ever in my life!

♥

When Shaun came back, he looked fresh and much lighter in comparison to before.

"Did you shower?" I asked as I saw his wet hair. He shrugged, bent and kissed me on my lips.

"You did not –" I started but he pressed his lips on mine once more.

"Shaun!" I complained.

"What?" he snapped, mood darkening again.

"Did you kill Ron?" I asked grimly.

"Couldn't get the pleasure yet, my security will take care of him," he barked, sitting back on my bed. "Are you feeling better? Meds kicking in?" he asked caressing my face.

"Did you kill Maria then?" I asked, perplexed.

"No, she is being deported to which ever sad place she came from," he shrugged. "She hardly knew what she was doing.

Ron was merely preying on her requirement for money. She has a very sick child back home!"

"Then what did you do?" I asked.

"Aren't you happy that I am feeling normal, even if slightly?" Shaun demanded.

I wanted to ask if he murdered the man who tried to rape me, but I couldn't muster the strength.

"Fine," I sighed. "By the way, not pregnant," I informed pointing at my tummy.

His face fell for a second, then he caressed my stomach lovingly and spoke, "Yeah, I found that out. I don't know what I would have done if you had, you know, lost our child!"

"Says the man who doesn't want a child," I snorted and the look he gave me rendered me mute.

"Who said I don't want a baby?" he shouted.

Someone knocked and entered. It was Daniel and Mia.

"Can I ever come and not find either of you shouting?" Daniel exclaimed but Shaun didn't pay heed to them.

"I said I don't want a kid just yet, especially before marriage, but I don't want to kill it if it is there," Shaun continued in the same raging tone.

"Oh-Em-Gee," Mia exclaimed, "Are you in here because you got an abortion? Mom is going to have such a fit," she laughed.

"Shut up!" both Shaun and I shouted.

Daniel took Mia to a side and filled her in.

"By the way, I postponed flights of your family to Friday," Shaun informed. "I gathered you don't want them to visit you in the hospital or while on bed rest, right?"

"Thank you," I agreed.

"But Simi will arrive tomorrow, so you will have your best friend, I thought you would want her in the present situation," he added.

And my eyes welled at his consideration.

"When can I go home?" I asked after a pause.

"Whenever you are feeling well enough," he stated.

"Right now then," I stressed. "And this is a stupid doctor, I am going to continue with the treatment the other one gave me."

"You fainted after her treatment," Shaun looked annoyed.

"I fainted because of stress," I corrected. "At least she didn't make up some miscarriage to gain sympathy of the billionaire!"

"Fine," he nodded and called someone asking to get me discharged.

"I think I should tell you one thing though, given everything and our wedding plans," I bit my lip as I hesitated.

"What?" he asked concerned.

I didn't know how to tell him this, but being honest was the best option. "Umm," I fiddled with the bed sheet.

"Hey," he sat beside me and grabbed my hand in encouragement.

I inhaled heavily and spoke, "The doctor, well the one I visited before, said that I've sustained severe injury to my uterus."

"I got as much, yes," Shaun nodded with a frown.

"The stab wound and yesterday..." I added.

"Will result in a difficult future pregnancy," Shaun finished.

My eyes were full of tears now. "I know we have not talked about having kids, but I know you want them. At some point, in years maybe, I too want them. But I may never have one!"

He wiped my face and spoke, "Science is advancing at a rapid rate. And if a person like me, in my position, cannot take the advantage of science and get the blessing of children, I don't think anyone can," he smiled simply.

When I didn't respond, he added, "If you won't be able to, we will get a surrogate. You don't have to worry about what may or may not happen. I don't care about kids just yet. All I care about is what you endured and how I can take care of you."

"Did you kill the man who attacked me?" Despite me resisting, the words came tumbling out of my mouth.

He gave me a look that said more than words, and then suddenly he smiled, "The only reason I am feeling sane is because I didn't just kill him, I tortured him to death."

Chapter 18

If my eyes could have popped open more with horror, they would have. How could he reply so serenely that he tortured a man to death!

Daniel who was listening to our conversation jumped in and spoke, "He is kidding, obviously."

I registered his attire as well.

"You too are showered," I pointed at his hair.

"Well, I think sometimes we all should bathe, don't we?" Daniel laughed.

"We both have showered because we got covered in the pervert bastard's blood and had to clean up as it would have raised awkward questions!" Shaun answered coolly.

My jaw dropped at these words as I imagined Shaun painted red.

"What are you doing?" Daniel hissed.

"I don't lie, Dan, you know it," Shaun replied. "Especially, to my family."

"Well, sometimes you should," Daniel stressed.

"Hmph," Shaun looked at me very seriously. "Last week, when I was in Brazil, I was attacked."

"What?" I asked, shocked.

"Yes, I was attacked and I came back to you not because of my security but because his security saved me," he pointed at Daniel, who couldn't believe Shaun. "A man there took an aim at me, grazed me with a bullet and ran away," and he undid his shirt and showed me his arm. I realized I had not seen him without a shirt since he came back. There was a bandage on his arm and Daniel grabbed his head in shock. "I tell my wife everything, Dan," Shaun added at his reaction.

"Oh my God," I spoke, holding him. "Are you okay? Why didn't you tell me? Does it hurt?" I asked as a sense of panic raced through me.

"I am fine now, didn't want to bother you when I was so far away," he caressed my face.

"Did you catch that man?" Mia asked, perplexed.

"Yes, did you? Was he punished?" I asked suddenly.

"No, I let him go," Shaun sighed.

"What?" I shouted. "You should have killed him, who was he? Why did he do it?"

"I didn't bother asking," his careless demeanour shocked me.

"Are you insane?" I shrieked. "If you don't punish such people, they will get a free reign to attack you. They will think they can do whatever they please and they can get away."

"Exactly," Shaun spoke flatly and took off the bandage from his arm and threw it away. There was no wound there.

"You were lying!" I gasped.

"No, I was illustrating," he growled. "A graze, and such reaction. And you are asking me why I tortured the man who raped you," he spoke through gritted teeth.

"I was not raped!" I repeated angrily.

Shaun inhaled loudly as if to calm himself. "No one, literally not one, lays hand on the women of my family. I gave one pass to Daksh," he spat, "but I am not going to let the man live who literally laid hands IN you!" he shouted the last two words.

"What do you mean by 'in you'?" Mia demanded, horrified. "That bastard did what to you?" she looked at me.

"Nothing he didn't regret till his last breath!" Shaun huffed as he stood up. "Now, I have some work to do, why don't you get dressed and head home, and I, well, I need to go and send a message to everyone that I won't take bullshit like this ever again," and he left with Daniel.

"I am thinking we do it in Brazil, rules are much relaxed over there," Daniel whispered as they walked out.

"What Brazil?" I asked quickly, "You are not leaving again, are you?"

Shaun turned and smiled. His demeanour was so casual that I was taken aback for a moment.

"It is too far away," Shaun spoke to Daniel without sparing him a glance. "Let it be here."

"What's here?" I asked again.

"You are here, my love," Shaun smiled and came back to kiss me on my lips. "I am not leaving you behind, ever again!"

"So where are you both going right now?" This time it was Mia who asked.

"Duty calls," he smiled at me. "I will be late today, just sleep if you feel tired," and with another kiss on my forehead, he left.

Mia, who was now alone with me, stared at me with pity and shock. The nurse came in and requested Mia to leave.

"Mind if I help you change?" Mia spoke, as she came in the curtain where the nurse was undoing my top.

The nurse stopped, but I nodded, and Mia too helped. The pain in my body was still there and I could hardly move. I didn't realize it before, but now it was evident.

"What did that bastard do to you?" Mia asked, staring at the scar on my stomach. It was now surrounded by a dark blue patch. The scar had opened on the inside when the bastard had kicked me and now I had internal bleeding.

"A few things," I sighed. "And this scar is my own doing."

"I heard about it," she sighed too. "You are crazier than I had thought."

I smiled at her sentiment.

The nurse helped me with my clothes and left. When alone, Mia said, "Don't blame Shaun, okay," she stressed. "He is used to getting his own way and usually his way is right."

"But…" I started.

"He showed you one fake bandage and you were so riled up, all willing to kill, he saw the video of that man raping you, imagine his condition," Mia whispered, combing my hair.

I felt shocked by her friendly behaviour. "Once, a man drugged me in a bar," she continued, "our security of course stopped him from doing anything but that man went missing that night. Till date I don't know what happened to that man but a person in our position, in Shaun's position, doesn't leave open ends, especially, when it comes to threats."

She pulled out her lipstick and started smearing my lips with it. I was so shocked that I didn't even stop her from painting me red. "A few men have gone missing over the years of my life, they all had tried to push themselves on me in some or the other way. People who threaten us don't see another day's light and that's how it is with us."

I just stared at her in shock.

"So if any man bumps into me, he dies?" I asked seriously.

"Not bump into you, silly," she tittered. "Any man who harms you or intends to harm you, dies."

"What happened to Ron?" I asked.

"Well, Ron's mother is running all over the globe to find whereabouts of her son, but I seriously think she should start scanning the oceans to find his remains," Mia shrugged. "I feel my brother is more agitated because he was not there to ensure everything is happening as per his will. He usually stays on top of everything, you see. But as you were attacked here, and given how new you are to our world, he could neither leave you behind nor take you with him!"

"Or maybe," Mia added thoughtfully, "ah yes, he first wanted to deal with the bastard here, then maybe take care of Ron."

I just gaped at her in shock. How easily were they talking about committing the serious crime!

"Think of it this way, justice has to be served, one way or another," Mia smiled finally. "Our Shauny just likes to deliver justice personally to people who do wrong to his women," and with that declaration, she walked out to ask for a wheelchair so that we both could head home.

Chapter 19

That day Shaun didn't come home but Mia didn't leave my side. I had a feeling she was keeping an eye on me but I didn't dare complain.

Owing to my injury, Sarina had transferred all my things to a room downstairs. "Mr Malani doesn't want you to take a lot of strain," she chirped as she handed me a new phone, "and this came after getting screened by the security."

"Ooh, your phone is an upgrade," Mia smiled as she checked out the device. "Hmm, maybe I too need a new phone," she said as she flipped her phone to the side and sat on my bed comfortably. "So what do you want to watch?" she asked and I just stared at the TV with a blank expression. "Oh, come on, there must be something we both could enjoy," she started flicking through show titles and chose one with a rich billionaire family and a brat daughter.

"Kind of our situation, isn't it?" Mia laughed. "Except Shaun is not my dad!" she rolled her eyes.

I smiled with her and quietly watched the show. I had watched a few episodes of this show before and to be honest, the brat daughter of the show always did remind me of Mia.

"You know they have based her on me?" Mia pointed at the brat daughter on the screen, "The writers told me, they took inspiration of clothing, style and look from me."

I supressed a giggle at this.

"I just think they made the girl a little too bratty, isn't it?" Mia wondered and I just couldn't control my laugh. I snorted and masked it with a cough, which resulted in a shooting pain and my eyes watered.

"Easy… alright," she spoke patting my back, "you can laugh openly if you like. I won't hold it against you. All my friends laugh at me because of this show!"

I looked away hopelessly.

"Anyway, do you think I am as bratty as this chick?" she pointed at the screen where the girl was having sex with the driver just to piss off her dad. "Although, I did do that," she pointed thoughtfully.

"With your driver?" I asked a bit normally now.

"Well, yeah!" she nodded casually. "What?" she added as despite my trying, a little judgment appeared on my face, "It was just sex."

"Umm, okay," I replied wondering how hooking up with random people was 'just sex'.

"As if you haven't done the dirty," she laughed. When I didn't respond to her, she sat up straight and looked at me intrigued.

"How many men have you been with?" she asked seriously and I just shrugged.

"Wow!" she mouthed. "So just my brother!"

I pouted. I knew I should say Daksh but didn't want to.

"But you were married before, weren't you?" she asked.

I nodded.

"Are you too embarrassed or too scared to talk freely?" she laughed.

"How many have you been with?" I asked curiously, hoping 'thousands' as Shaun spoke the other day was not true.

"Eh! I don't keep a count," she just flipped her hair and lay back on the mountain of pillow, "Like I said, it is just sex."

"But still," I started. "I mean how!"

"How?" she raised her eyebrows. "Oh, I don't swing that way to tell you how sex works, but I am sure my brother will be very happy to give you a crash course," she laughed raucously.

"I mean, why with so many men?" I corrected my statement.

"Because I could, and well, we all should. How would you know if what you are getting from one is good or even enough!" she rolled her eyes and my jaw dropped. "I mean, your ex, how did you know that it was the best sex you were having? Well, when my brother came along he did prove you wrong, didn't he?"

I felt my face burn at this.

"Oh, my brother is very good, I know that," she laughed.

I blinked rapidly at this, so she added, "I have heard, girls go wild when with him. We have many times shared adjoining rooms on trips," she laughed and I felt furious. How could she speak about her brother like that!

"Not every man is an animal in bed, you know," she shrugged. "I have found, I guess ten maybe fifteen who are satisfactory," she twirled her hand dramatically.

I opened my mouth but couldn't find a single word to say to her. She and I belonged in so different worlds... was it the way they were raised or was it because of the money they grew up in? Will my children be like this too?

She was staring at me with mock admiration, so I was forced to ask, "So out of all the infinite men you had slept with, you didn't find one you found worthy of love?"

"Love?" and she laughed so loudly that I almost jumped in bed. "Don't you think love is nothing but a little overrated feeling?"

"Actually, no!" I replied.

"Shaun fell in love with you, after being with God knows how many women, and look where it has landed him," she snorted.

"Where has Shaun landed?" I asked seriously.

"He has cried more than a dozen times since he fell in love with you. Believe me it is a big thing because that man doesn't shed a tear for anyone," she sighed.

"A dozen? When?" I asked, alarmed.

"Well, I think the first time was when you both were in Australia, he was so devastated that I had to fly down there over the weekend to comfort him," she looked annoyed at the memory. "He was really down that time, it was a mammoth task to bring him back to London, you know!" she rolled her eyes at this.

"I didn't know," I whispered as I imagined a depressed Shaun.

"How could you? He doesn't tell you anything that might upset you. He feels it is his job to protect you," she smiled. "Well, we all protect the people we love," she shrugged carelessly.

"But wasn't Shaun in India?" I asked, remembering how he appeared at Marine Drive when Daksh had hit me.

"Yeah, he was. He stayed home for less than a day. Though you were not together at the time, he didn't want to live half-way across the world, so he flew back the evening I brought him back to London," she informed.

"Then he cried when you stabbed yourself, you are such a stupid person. I felt so annoyed that I didn't bother coming down. Mom did though," Mia shrugged carelessly. "Mom too wasn't impressed by your actions, but well, given how Shaun was, she had to accept you."

"Had to accept me?" I asked with narrowed eyes.

"Well yeah! She didn't expect the girl Shaun loves to be married to someone else. I mean affair and all aside, people do take being already married a bit in a negative way, don't you think?" Mia wondered and I bit my lip. I really was in no mood to argue with her.

"Shaun cried a lot around those days. And he has shed gallons of tears in the last two days," she finished. "How often have you cried for him?"

I looked at her but didn't reply.

"You haven't cried a lot over him, have you?" Mia asked. "I think Shaun makes you stronger. Your tears over cheating on your ex aside, you don't cry because of Shaun. But it is other way around for men like Shaun!"

"What do you mean?" I asked suddenly.

"I mean Shaun is one of the most powerful men in the world. And you make him so weak that punk like Ron found a way to hurt him. And know when I say it, Ron has been trying to get to Shaun for years now. They both never saw eye-to-eye, hence Shaun gave him Australia so that he lived the farthest from him. But through you, Ron found his weakness. Ron realized how vulnerable you make Shaun when you went to Australia with him and just at one word from you, Shaun took the day off and went away with you on a sight-seeing trip."

I didn't know what to say to this. It felt like she was blaming me for Shaun's misery.

"How do you know all this?" I asked, trying to mask my disappointment.

"Shaun and I are closer than you know," she laughed. "He tells me everything, including what Ron told Shaun this morning."

"What did Ron tell him this morning?" I asked now very seriously.

"Shaun had Ron picked up last night, so he must be landing in a few hours in London," Mia informed. "Flight between London and Sydney is just way too long, I could never sit in a plane for so long!" she rolled her eyes and I waited for her to continue. "When your maid confessed and identified Ron as the person who was paying her, Shaun finally talked to Ron, while he was still in the air. Of course, Ron had no other choice but to confess to everything."

I waited eagerly for her to continue; her dramatic pauses were getting on my nerves but I was resisting.

"I was all up for throwing him overboard, but Shaun decided otherwise," Mia shrugged.

"Where is Shaun right now?" I asked, panicking.

"I don't know, do I? I am here with you," she shrugged again. "Do you have a filer?" she asked staring at her perfect nails.

"But Shaun said his security took care of Ron," I continued.

"He is not going to leave Ron alone until he is dead, believe me," she snorted. "I think I need to book a nail appointment," she added thoughtfully.

"But you said he was agitated that he was not there to ensure everything is done properly and Ron's mom should search the oceans," I spoke, confused.

"Umm, did I?" Mia pouted. "Hold on!" and she dialled a number.

"Where are you?" Mia demanded as someone answered her call.

Pause!

"Ahaa," she nodded.

Pause!

"Ahaa," she smiled.

Pause!

"Ahaa," she spoke in a jovial tone and I felt my anger rise.

"Can I come to let out a bit of frustration myself?" she asked in an excited voice.

"Is he with Ron?" I asked quickly but she just shook her head.

"Fine, so you will have all the fun while I stay here and girl-talk your fiancée?" she demanded.

Pause!

"Yeah, fair enough," she nodded, and disconnected.

I just stared at her.

"Yep, he is having just too much fun and he will be back later, he wants me to pass on his love to you and tell you to go to sleep," she spoke jumping out of bed.

"Where are you going?" I asked suddenly as Mia walked to the door.

"To get security to pick up my nail artist, I am just not happy with my hands right now," and with one long assessing look at her hands, she walked out.

Chapter 20

After having that illuminating conversation with Mia, I decided to sleep. She came back and watched the TV show we had started watching together, then she went to get her nails done.

When I woke up the next morning, I found my bed empty. Neither Shaun, nor Mia were there. However, Sarina was instantly beside me the moment I opened my eyes.

"Do you have some kind of sensor to know I am awake?" I smiled as she helped me sit up.

She laughed affectionately and handed me my breakfast in bed and pills. Ideally, I would brush my teeth but given the pain I had, she insisted I ate a bit and took my meds first.

Once, I had obeyed her, she spoke with motherly affection, "Mr Malani asked me to pass on his regards to you and said he will be back before lunch. And, if you are up for it, you have a visitor," Sarina informed.

"Visitor?" I asked, confused.

"I will send her in then," and taking the tray from my bedside, she went out. I stared at the door expectantly and then she came.

"Simi," I gasped as I saw my best friend stand in the doorway. "Oh my God, Simi," I cried as I raised my hands and she hurried and threw herself in my arms.

From her face it looked like she had been crying and was anxious.

"When did you arrive?" I asked after a few minutes.

"Early this morning," she informed, sniffing slightly.

"Then why didn't any one wake me up?" I complained.

"Well, I was taken straight to lover boy's office," she informed, sitting comfortably on my bed. "Then I was brought here but your maids didn't let me come. She said you were resting and you were not to be disturbed," she rolled her eyes. "I wanted to fight but given what has happened, I decided to wait."

"What happened?" I asked, shocked.

"Why do you think lover boy called me to his office," Simi paused, "Oh, Kaya," and she flung herself on me again.

"I am fine, was he fine?" I asked seriously.

"He looked okay," Simi shrugged.

I was a little surprised by this but it was kind of good that he was okay!

"I guess committing murder helps calm him down," I sighed.

"Yeah, it would calm me down," Simi agreed.

"He told you?" I asked sharply.

"No, I demanded if he killed the person who raped you and he said rather harshly that 'of course', like I was insulting him by even asking the question," Simi laughed.

"I was not raped!" I corrected again.

"I know, and I am so grateful," and she prayed silently. "Good thing he arrived just in time. I will love him forever for this."

"So he really murdered that man," I whispered.

"And this guy called Ron who was the mastermind behind it all," Simi informed.

"How are you okay with it?" I barked.

"Remember when in college, that fifth year molested me," Simi started.

"How can I forget? If only I had the power, I would have –" I paused abruptly.

"Well, your lover boy does have the power and he did. If you want to avenge your friend's honour by committing a murder, then why won't he?" she demanded.

"Wanting and doing are different things," I snapped.

"The only line between wanting and doing is the means and courage. Appreciate his love and the extent to which he would go for you, and stop bitching about what happened. Now your future is bright and shiny, stay happy forever."

I didn't reply to this so she added, "When is the wedding then?"

"I don't know!" I sighed.

"And what else is new," she asked.

And I told her all about my conversation with Mia yesterday. Her jaw dropped at my words.

"Shut up!" she giggled as she registered. "By the way, come to think of it, she is right, isn't it!"

"About what?" I asked.

"Well, how would I know if I am getting the best sex of my life," she giggled again. "You got with lover boy, but me..." and she pouted.

"Oh, shut up," and I hit her with the pillow and we laughed.

As I was so close to Simi, we sometimes discussed a few things related to sex and as I blushed, she said, "Oh, you are making me so insecure. I wish Rahul would lock me with him for a few hours only and just focus on me! But eh! Our men are just useless when it comes to romance, isn't it?"

"Well, if gotten his way, Shaun would never leave the room," I snickered.

"Were you always this good or is it lover boy's doing?" she elbowed me and I blushed.

"Ahem! Hmm!"

We looked up and saw Shaun standing there.

"Am I the lover boy you are discussing or someone else?" he asked with a laugh.

I pressed my face in my palms and snickered.

"May I have a moment with her," Shaun asked Simi.

"If only that moment won't stretch to days," she giggled.

He huffed, then spoke, "I may have said 'yes, it could' but in her present condition, no, you are safe," he laughed loudly.

Simi got up, hugged him tightly, whispered something in his ears and left.

"What was that?" I asked, laughing still.

"She is just happy to see you happy," he replied, sitting on the bed. He lifted my shirt and stared at my wound. "I hope you are feeling better," he sighed.

"I am," I nodded.

"And do you forgive me?" he asked sincerely.

"For what?" I asked.

"For committing the crimes that is not letting you rest," he expressed. It was impressive how he didn't utter the word 'murder'.

"I understand, so let's never discuss it again, okay!" I stressed.

"Perfect," and he grinned broadly. "So bringing your BFF was the right decision after all."

"The best one," I grinned too.

"Always keep smiling, my love," and he kissed me with warmth. He started to pull back but I grabbed his coat and pulled him closer. "Where do you think you are going?" I whispered huskily.

He kissed me deeply but then let my hands drop.

"No extra-curriculars until your insides are healed, okay," he poked my nose.

"But I want more!" I groaned.

He grinned broadly at this and pressed his lips firmly on mine again. Instinctively I moved, and winced.

He drew back and looked at me.

"I want more too, but these painful winces are sore buzz killer," he didn't smile this time, he looked very concerned.

I pouted and bit my lower lip.

"A little longer," he whispered. "And something tells me holding back before marriage makes honeymoon even more enticing," he bit my lower lip again and I blushed.

"Two to three weeks is doctor's orders. So let's wait till our honeymoon," he laughed now.

"Can I come in?" Simi returned with her hands shielding her eyes. "Is it safe for me to open my eyes," she mocked.

"One second," I replied and pulled him closer again.

"I have counted till fifty now, you know," she laughed and Shaun drew back.

"I will take your leave, ladies," he spoke. "And yes, child, you can look at adults in here now," he mocked.

Simi giggled as she sat on my bed.

"You can stay back and spend time with me, you know," Simi said, "I am not that bad a company!"

"You are the best company, but I am needed elsewhere presently," he sighed. "I will see you later then," and getting up, he planted another peck on my lips and left.

Chapter 21

I spent the next two weeks healing and getting better. Witnessing my health, Shaun had postponed my parents travel and now they were arriving later. Simi helped out a lot in many things, especially, things related to wedding.

Coming from Indian background, a white wedding was a new thing for us, and we both were epically excited. But neither was my mother, nor was Shaun's.

The evening my family arrived, Shaun's mother also graced us with her presence in Airia.

"Why are you so pale?" was my mother's first comment. "Doesn't she look pale?" she asked my father. He did look a bit concerned as he looked at me but didn't comment.

"We all think our children are getting weak if they are not living under our roof," Shaun's mother laughed. My mother laughed too, and something told me both our moms were either going to be best friends or they were going to be stark enemies!

As everyone settled in their rooms, Shaun was called in. He had been avoiding me slightly since our last encounter. He requested Simi to sleep in with me while he lived in the room upstairs. This arrangement made my mother exceptionally happy because first thing she did was scan through my room to ensure Shaun was not living with me! Which at the moment was not the case.

I felt my heart jerk when I saw him arrive. I don't think I would ever get used to his sudden arrivals.

"You are drooling," he snickered as he sat on the sofa next to me and I adjusted my face.

"This is the most I have seen you in the past couple of days," I complained in a whisper. "I missed you."

"Have to do so much if I want a long break for our honeymoon, isn't it?" he muttered.

I felt my heart skip beats at the words 'long break'.

I was about to say something when his mother cleared her throat and we looked towards her. "I believe it was *I* who called you here to talk, Shaun!" she started.

Shaun sat up straight and looked at her with mild curiosity. "Didn't you say you only have a few minutes to spare for me?" his mother demanded.

"I did say that and it is a fact," Shaun replied simply.

"So let's discuss the points on hand," his mother narrowed her eyes and Shaun sighed and nodded.

"I am appalled by the fact that despite my specific request, you are getting married the wrong way!" she started and my mother's face lit up.

"Yes, I agree, this is all wrong," my mother chirped too.

"What's wrong, mother?" he asked seriously.

"The day is wrong, the time is wrong, the venue is wrong, and of course, the type of wedding is wrong," his mother dictated. "The auspicious time of getting married for you is 22nd November."

"Who said that?" Shaun demanded.

"*Pandit ji,*" my mother added with big-round eyes. "I showed both of yours *patrika* to a big *pandit* in India, he said *dev so rahe hain,* if you will get married without God's blessings, your marriage will be cursed."

Shaun and I stared at my mother's stupefied expressions for a moment. He then turned to me, and I very quickly translated her Hindi words for him. He listened to me for a second, then without any cue, he started laughing.

My mother's expression changed from shock to offence.

"Shaun!" his mother barked, "Have you no respect for your future mother-in-law?"

"Respect for her?" he spoke between guffaws, "I mean yes, but not for these views."

"These are my views too," his mother spoke stiffly.

Snorting derisively, Shaun spoke, "I don't care whose views they are. People get married round the clock in the world. Are all the marriages cursed just because your *Gods are sleeping?* I mean come on, Gods sleeping, really!"

"Shaun," I spoke and placed my hand on his.

"I won't take it," he shook his head at this.

"Please, these are our moms, we have to respect their views. This is our culture," I tried to reason.

He stood up angrily at this. "We are getting married on the day we have planned," he spoke as he looked at me.

"I don't accept it," his mother spat. "What is the hurry?"

"Well, mother," he spoke as he buttoned his coat, a gesture that said the meeting was over from his side, "I love her and I am not going to leave her behind again ever. And to take her with me on non-stop business trips, I have to get her a British passport, everything is in place except for the damn marriage certificate. So I am getting married," he then turned to my mother, "I know you don't appreciate us living in the same room."

My mother stared at him in disbelief, so he added, "I have booked a rather long honeymoon starting in the following week, so –"

"Okay-okay, I knew you were a ghoul," my mother muttered.

"Mother!" I shouted.

"If you ladies will please excuse me, I have many things to plan for my wedding," and he started to walk out.

"Shaun!" I spoke, and he turned. "Please!" I requested as I pointed at the seat beside me.

He came back and sat much closer to me. My mother's mouth twisted.

"Would you like it if your mom hates me and my mom hates you?" I whispered.

"I actually don't care," he replied.

"I care, so?" I demanded.

He stared at me with same angry look and I glared back at him, while all others stared at us with mixed expressions.

"Fine," Shaun made a face as he looked at me. "Fine!" he snapped again. "22nd November it is," he growled.

"At least one of you have some sense," his mother spoke.

"22nd November will be the Indian wedding, but the day after tomorrow we will be getting married are per the plan," he finished, and I slapped my forehead. "One way or another, you are taking the Malani name this week, so we will do both weddings, deal?" he asked his mother.

"*Bin phere hum tere,*" my mother growled. Simi, Arsh and I giggled at her words.

"What is she muttering?" Shaun asked, perplexed, and I shook my head.

"Two weddings?" his mother raised her eyes to the heavens and Simi laughed out loud.

Everyone stared at her so she spoke, "I just remembered you had threatened me, 'Don't you dare miss my last wedding!'"

I closed my eyes in exasperation.

"Still not happy?" he asked me. "Weren't you yourself planning this wedding for the last weekend? I don't know what you people want!"

"We want you to be happy," his mother started.

"Do I look happy to you, mother? I was happy when I entered this room, but do I look happy now?" he raged.

"What should we do then?" It was Simi who added.

"We can vote," Arsh supplied.

"Cool," Shaun barked, "our marriage and others get to vote, simply splendid."

"Vote of your family, Shaun!" his mother snapped too.

"All in favour of this weekend marriage because that would make Kaya and me happy," Shaun spoke through gritted teeth.

My father, Arsh, Simi and Shaun raised their hands. Shaun glared at me.

"All in favour of wedding on 22nd November," Shaun barked.

Shaun's mother, my mother, Arsh and my father raised their hands.

"What?" Arsh spoke, "Two weddings sound like an amazing plan," he laughed.

"It is a tie," Simi sighed and all of them looked at me.

"I am either not voting or voting on both," I raised both my hands in defence.

"Fine," Shaun snapped, "I have one more family member," he spoke and dialled Mia's number. Shaun's mother looked appalled.

"Mia, I need your vote," Shaun spoke on the call while everyone else heard on speaker.

"Fine," Mia spoke uninterestedly, "what do you want me to say and where?"

"Good," Shaun smiled. "Kindly say, 'I vote for this weekend'," he spoke.

"This weekend?" Mia laughed, "your wife would kill you if you planned something on your wedding day!"

"You are voting for our wedding day; it is either this weekend or 22nd November in India!"

"Weekend it is," she chirped and Shaun disconnected.

"Votes done, and case is closed. And you," he pointed at me, "How are you feeling?" he demanded.

"Fine," I shrugged. "Why?"

"Because I am getting very angry now!" and with one look that said Simi was not going to sleep in my room tonight, he left.

Chapter 22

Mia came in the evening and dragged Simi and me out for drinks.

"Where are we going?" Simi asked curiously.

"She is getting married the day after tomorrow, don't you want to give your friend proper send off to the wedded bliss?" Mia demanded as we entered a club.

"Oh yes, but she doesn't drink, you know!" Simi laughed as we met a few of Mia's girlfriends and felt exceptionally awkward. Mia's friend circle was so different from us. We knew it was a party, so Simi and I were dressed in knee length dresses, however, her friends, well, I had no description for them.

"Oh really?" Mia looked at me curiously. "Let's see now," and one of her friends brought a tray from the bar counter filled with shot glasses and Mia pressed one shot glass in my hand and one in Simi's.

"Here is to future Mrs Shaun Malani," Mia shouted at the top of her voice, and everyone drank. I looked around, and as Mia glared at me, I raised my glass to her and drank and choked.

"What is this?" Simi asked seriously.

"I don't know," Mia laughed. Everyone else was standing still, while my head swam.

"Okay?" Simi asked me seriously.

"Are you going to pass out right in the beginning of your bachelor party?" Mia demanded, agitated.

I just smiled.

"Wow, you are a light drinker," Mia's voice was full of sarcasm. "Another round –" she shouted and one more tray appeared. And while everyone raised their glasses, Simi drank hers, swapped with me and drank mine too.

"That's my girl," Mia snickered as she saw the empty glass in my hand.

"Stay sober or your lover boy will kill me," Simi muttered.

"You too, or your husband will kill me," I replied.

"You know me, I am not gonna fall after a few shots," Simi shrugged. And it was true. Since college days, Simi was a tanker. Once she drank the whole night, wrote paper the next day and passed with flying colours.

"Let's take this party to a little private corner," Mia laughed and placing a tiara on my head and sash that said 'Bride to be' across my torso, she pushed me in a party chamber.

My head swam as I tried to focus on what was up ahead. I stood rooted to the ground as the music began and a few boys - very handsome, very muscly boys started dancing on a stage.

"Come now," Mia laughed as she pushed me ahead.

"What is happening?" I asked Simi seriously.

"Apparently this is your send off to your marital bliss," Simi too had her mouth hanging open now. "What kind of bachelor parties these people have?" she wondered.

Mia pushed me in a chair while all her friends scattered around. They were hooting at the boys, and as if being spurred on, all boys were shaking their bodies savagely.

The boy in the centre spotted the tiara and sash around me and winked in my direction. My eyes popped open as he jumped from the stage and danced his way towards me.

"Dance with him," Mia giggled. "Maybe you will get to experience one more before you get tied to my brother for life."

"What?" I shrieked over the music.

"Kidding, I know Shaun would kill both you and me," she laughed as the boy grabbed my hand and made me stand up. He bowed in front of me while another boy from stage came in and pushed another shot on my lips. I tried to stop him, but the boy in the lead pressed his fingers in my cheek, and I drank.

I drank one. I drank another. By the time I was on my sixth shot, everything was shifting.

"Now, that's my girl," the lead boy snickered as he hoisted me on his shoulder and took me to the centre stage.

I could hear Mia's laugh, her friends' titters but I was just too fazed to do anything.

"Ensure she doesn't fall," Simi shouted from a distance and I felt the lead boy's hand around my waist.

I pushed his hand away and before I could do anything, I heard a cloth tear. I turned, and though everything was fuzzy, I saw his shirt appear in front of my face. I pushed it aside and now he stood in front of me shirt less.

The lead boy held my hand and grabbed my waist and started twirling me in his arms. "Loosen a bit, darling, this is your last night of freedom," he laughed.

"What?" I asked, alarmed.

"I think she needs another shot," the lead laughed.

"NO! Stop!" I heard Simi shriek. "DO SOMETHING!" she yelled at someone.

"Oh, come now, darling," the lead was laughing as he pushed me down on my knees and made me undo his belt. As I realized what was happening, I pulled my hand and I felt another something fall on my lips.

"No…" I started to say but someone else grabbed my shoulders.

"Ms Pradhan," It was David, "Are you okay?"

"Shaun!" I whispered.

"Mr Malani is not here," David spoke as he tried to help me up.

"I want Shaun here," I whispered again. "Call him here."

"Oh, get out of the way, it is her bachelor party," Mia shouted.

But David didn't move.

"Her safety is my priority," David was saying. "No other man is to land a hand on her!"

Everyone around was muttering now.

"And what was I doing, baiting her to the wolves?" Mia barked.

"What happened?" another voice came, but before him came his security. "Are you alright?"

"Oh, the fiancé is here too," the lead shouted, but one look at David's face and Shaun's security, he stepped back.

"Is she okay?" Shaun asked quickly.

"You are here?" I asked as he sat in front of me and looked at me.

"You asked me to be here," he smiled, "so I had to come, isn't it?"

"Oh," and without any further ado, I grabbed his collar and kissed him. Everyone around howled and cheered as I kissed him fiercely.

"What are you doing? And how drunk are you?" he demanded as he pushed me back.

"Having my husband," I smiled and he raised his eyebrows.

"You know what?" I slurred.

"I will know when we are out of here," he muttered.

"You look so sexy when you do this," and I squinted my eyes to raise my eyebrows.

"What?" he asked, alarmed. "Why did you drink so much?" he demanded.

"She didn't, they made her," Simi pointed at the stage.

"You girls hired strippers?" Shaun barked.

"Ooh, are they strippers? I have never seen one, Simi have you seen one," I snickered as I turned and looked around. "No wonder he wanted me to take his pants off."

"What?" Shaun roared and Mia squealed, "You should take her home, bro."

"You threw my wife to strippers," Shaun growled.

"Well, we all were here to take care of her. I wouldn't have let her do anything, maybe a kiss or something," Mia shrugged. "Oh, let her enjoy."

"MIA," Shaun shouted.

"*Ooye!*" I shouted too, "She is my sister now, don't shout at my sister, you mister."

Mia snickered, "How light weight is she?"

"She doesn't drink!" Shaun informed.

"I can see," Mia laughed. "Hey, Kaya," she added, "try this," and she lit a cigarette and passed on to me. But Shaun took it instead.

"Aww… you are so adorable when you are so fucking overprotective," I jeered and with the cigarette in Shaun's hands, I blew it and choked.

"Enjoy, brother," Mia laughed and turned to continue her party, while I just clung to Shaun, massaging his shoulders, chest, back.

He looked so taken aback that he just stared at me.

"I want you," I hissed in his ears. "Right now!" and pushing my hand on his ass, I pushed him on me.

"Kaya," Simi pulled me back, "we are in public," she scolded.

"Oh, Simi, I love you," and I pulled her close and kissed her on the lips. She just sat rooted to the ground.

Shaun pulled me away, hoisted me on his shoulders and said, "It would be best to lock you up today." And with that, we all left the party.

♥

"Simi," Shaun spoke.

"I am going to come in Kaya's car, you carry on in yours," Simi tried to mask her laugh as she walked after David to my car, while Shaun placed me in his.

"What did they give you?" Shaun asked perplexed as he sat next to me and I got up and sat on him. "Drive, just drive," Shaun ordered his driver.

I pressed my lips on his and raked his hair with my fingers. "Have you ever done it in a moving car?" I asked in his ears.

He looked like he was confounded for a second.

"You have, haven't you?" I asked, feeling agitated.

"What are you doing?" he demanded. "I will kill Mia. And drive faster, okay!" he ordered and I felt the driver push his foot down on the accelerator.

His phone buzzed, "Yes," he answered.

"Are you taking her home?" I heard Simi's voice.

"Yes, oh crap!" Shaun cursed. "Re-route to Presidency Hotel," he spoke to the driver.

"Good, and what am I to say to her mother, who is waiting for her at home?" Simi demanded.

"Tell her she went to office for some urgent work," Shaun spoke.

"Oh, I do have some urgent work," I moaned in his ears.

"Oh my God!" Simi laughed. "Is that really her?"

"What did they give her?" Shaun demanded as I slid my hands between his legs and his eyes popped open. "How would I take her inside the hotel in this condition. If someone took a photo or a video, I am done."

"I can take us to the back entrance," the driver suggested.

"Good, check us in in advance," Shaun agreed and the driver made some calls.

"Well, you enjoy letting out your anger from the day, I will face her parents alone," Simi laughed.

"You understood?" Shaun asked, shocked.

"We are BFFs, lover boy. I know what your 'anger' and 'pent up energy' means," she laughed again.

"You girls," and laughing with Simi, he disconnected.

Shaun carried me in his arms to a room in the hotel, and while his security swept the room, he placed me on the bed.

Sitting up in bed, I started unzipping my dress but Shaun held my hands. "Stop!" he hissed and looked at the men who were sweeping the room, "She is drugged," he explained to the room at large.

They checked the room, gave him a nod and went away. Shaun rushed to the door, locked it, took off his coat and turned, "Now, what do you want to do?"

"I am a naughty, *such a naughty* girl," I snickered.

"Then, let's punish you."

♥

As I opened my eyes the next morning, I felt screeching pain in my temples.

"What?" I sat up straight as I took stock of my surroundings. "Oh crap!" fear gripped me as I registered my nakedness.

Tears leaked my eyes as I heard the bathroom flush.

I picked up my phone and called Shaun who answered on the first ring, "I don't know how, but something –" I sniffed, "I think, I did something incredibly wrong. Please forgive –" and he walked out of the bathroom, looking perplexed.

"You are here?" I whispered as I looked at him in his towel.

"Yeah, I am here," he shrugged. "And for which wrongful deed am I forgiving you?" he asked.

"Oh, thank God!" and I fell back in the bed grabbing my head. "I thought I slept with one of the men on stage."

"Well, you didn't. But were you planning to?" he laughed as he passed me the hangover cure.

"I don't remember much, what happened last night?" I asked.

"Let's not embarrass you more," he laughed again. "But I do want to tell you that you do need to get high more often."

"Why?" I asked seriously.

"Because, I would love to see this wild side of you again and again," and he snickered.

"I don't even remember last night," I bit my lip.

"Oh, I remember every second of it," and he laughed again, and he kept on laughing for so long that his eyes watered.

"What did I do?" I asked, panicking.

"You asked David to call me," Shaun informed. "I love it that even in your full drunken state, you want me."

"Of course, I would want only you!" I snapped.

"And you made dangerous passes at me in public. You were so high, you… well, I had to carry you here through back exit because I couldn't dare take you to the front door. I didn't want to appear in the headlines just before our wedding," he guffawed.

"Oh GOD!" I exclaimed.

"Oh, you remembered God a lot when we were alone in this room. I didn't know you had this side in you," he grinned and I closed my eyes in humiliation. "There is nothing wrong in having some ravaged sex with your future husband, you know!"

"It is wrong when you don't remember a second of it," I barked.

"Maybe I will record it the next time," he teased. "I need to know what Mia gave you."

"I will kill your sister," I growled.

"I was going to kill her too, but after last night, she gets a thank you card from my side," and he laughed loudly.

Punching him, I took a quick shower and got dressed.

"What did you tell my mother?" I demanded as we stepped out.

"Well, Simi told her you were called to work. And because she was calling you non-stop, I turned off your phone sometime in the middle of the night," he informed.

I glared at him and checked the missed calls – *more than forty*. I gulped and sat in his car.

"Today is our wedding rehearsal," Shaun grinned as he planted a kiss on my lips. "I don't think you could have made me happier today."

I looked at the driver and security men sitting up front. For the first time, they too had a small smile on their faces.

"You seduced me in front of them while they drove us to the hotel," Shaun snickered in my ears. I closed my eyes in embarrassment.

"I was drugged," I spoke. I tapped on their shoulders and spoke with as much dignity as possible, "I was drugged. My apologies for my behaviour last night."

"We understand, ma'am," the driver spoke mechanically.

Chapter 23

My mother was beside herself when I arrived with Shaun. She was red with rage. My father looked worried but he had accepted my life by now.

"You, where were you?" my mother demanded. "Why didn't you come home last night?"

I had no answer to it.

"We were working," Shaun replied. My mother looked at his dishevelled clothes and they said everything. Where Shaun was always impeccably dressed, now his tie was in his pocket, top buttons of his shirt were open, and his coat was hanging lose.

"Like this?" my mother pointed and he just shrugged.

"I am going for a shower, you too should head to the bathroom. We are off for the wedding rehearsal in a few hours," and with a kiss on my cheek, he jogged upstairs.

"You spent the night with him?" my mother demanded.

"I don't know where I spent the night mother," I replied.

"What do you mean?" my mother demanded again.

"That I am an adult, I can do whatever I feel like. I didn't do anything wrong, so please, I have a massive headache and I have no strength to answer you at present," I replied, and giving her cold, horrified face one last look, I walked away.

♥

"What kind of weddings are these?" my mother muttered as we sat in a big hall. "They need rehearsals!" she spat.

"Mother!" I scolded as the wedding planner – who was acting as a minister for the rehearsal – glared at her.

Shaun arrived with Daniel and a few of his friends, and everyone took their positions. Shaun stood in front of the minister, while Daniel stood beside Shaun, and Simi stood just next to the spot I was supposed to take. Arsh stood with a small plate which was supposed to hold the rings.

Heaving a sigh, my dad patted his thighs twice and got up and both of us stepped out of the room.

"Shall we?" I asked him with a smile as I saw Mia enter the hall before us. It looked like she was gliding and I wondered how I would look walking just behind her!

My father nodded and I placed my hand in his and we walked inside.

"I think mom is exceptionally unhappy with this," I muttered as my eyes fell on her. I was supposed to look at Shaun and smile, but my eyes lingered on her instead.

"She is not able to get over her old-school teachings, that's all," my father informed. "And your relationship with Shaun is not helping too."

I faltered in my steps at these words. He steadied me as I saw Shaun making a move to support me. Shaun stopped, seeing me stand straight. "I get it you are an adult and you, well, you can do what you want. I like Shaun so, despite my reservations, I don't say much, but give some leeway to your mother," he continued.

I felt embarrassed as he spoke this. Anyways, tonight was the last night and then tomorrow, we would be married so all would be 'legal' anyway.

"Also," my father grinned this time, "I think she is feeling a bit left out as we all are part of this wedding but she is not," and patting me lovingly on my head, he gave my hand to Shaun, who took with a beaming smile.

The acting minister started to speak, but it was more of instructions as to what was to happen tomorrow.

"Then you will exchange your vows, then rings, then final kiss, and then you will be married. Anyone has any questions?" the acting minister mainly asked me.

I shook my head wondering if Shaun had prepared vows for tomorrow.

Then we were ushered to a table where we had some wine, I took just a few sips only when people toasted to us. We had our dinner and then left for the day.

"You are going to have super fun tomorrow," Daniel laughed as we all stepped back in Airia.

My mother, who was exceptionally quiet since her rehearsal remark, moved to her room quietly. I knocked and entered.

"I am sorry," I started, "for upsetting you on so many things, I am sorry."

She didn't look at me but continued to check her dress.

"Mom," I started again, "would you at least pretend you are happy for me?"

"I—" she started but stopped abruptly.

"Fine," I sighed and started to go but she spoke suddenly, "It is not that I am not happy for you, you are my daughter I am happy but I cannot understand why you chose someone like him?"

"Like him?" I asked.

"Not an Indian? He is not one of us. He is a foreigner, and we all know what their values are," she continued.

"He loves me," I explained.

"And I remember you loving Daksh just as much as you think you love him," she pointed at the door. "I still remember the day when you married Daksh. I had never seen you so happy, but then –"

"Then I fell out of love. Daksh and I both stopped loving each other after a while," I reasoned.

"But you would never have left Daksh and would have continued to try if *he* had not shown up. He manipulated you," she added.

"I stopped trying with Daksh long before Shaun came, mom," I sighed. "You always thought Daksh was the perfect son, perfect husband. You never understood our issues."

"Well, there is no use now. I know Daksh loves that girl he is marrying, so there is no hope for you getting back with him," she continued as if I had not said a word in between.

"What do you want from me then? To go back to Daksh?" I exclaimed.

"I do, but he won't take you now," she sighed and I felt anger rise in me again.

"So you would have me go back to unhappy, miserable, loveless life and marriage but not live happily with Shaun?" I demanded.

"He will stop loving you," she whispered. "If Daksh and you could, then what would stop this Shaun of yours!"

And tears filled my eyes at these words.

"Am I so horrible, unlovable that you think even Shaun would fall out of love with me?" I asked sadly.

"I don't want to see you sad and alone," she muttered.

"I am not unlovable," I almost shouted this time.

"I am not saying that," she retorted.

"What's happening?" my father asked as he entered, followed by Shaun.

"Fine, mom," I raised my hands, "accept this marriage, reject this marriage. Love me. Hate me. Do whatever you feel like, just don't pray or believe or whatever that Shaun would also stop loving me like Daksh did. And mind you, I am warning you, this is the last time you are taking Daksh's side. He is out of my life. He is not my husband anymore. So he is not your son-in-law anymore. Shaun is. So appreciate the way he loves me and stop comparing him with the man who didn't love your daughter enough to fight for her!"

"Easy," Shaun spoke as he rubbed my arms to calm me.

"What are you doing?" my father spoke to my mother. "Why would you upset her by bringing up Daksh a night before her wedding?"

"I won't break your daughter's heart, I promise," Shaun spoke to my mother. "Despite what you feel for me, I love her, more than you can imagine. However, given what you think about me, I hope I will be able to show you over the course of our lives."

My mother didn't respond to his beautiful words. I turned and hugged him and he whispered in my ears, "Just one more day, my love. Just one more day…"

The Last One

The wedding morning arrived and the whole house was on fire, not literally, but preparatory way.

Since morning there was confuffle in the house, but I didn't care. I knew all will be well, and right after breakfast, Simi and I were driven to the wedding destination. The venue was a cute little B&B by the beach.

As we all gathered in the hall of the B&B, we all were asked to board.

"Board?" Simi asked, half excited, half shocked.

I just shrugged and Daniel appeared and informed that the venue has arrived.

"Arrived?" Arsh laughed and shouted as he looked out the window, "It is a cruise liner."

My jaw dropped as we all walked out and went to the dock to board.

"I thought we were getting married in the chapel here?" I spoke to Daniel who was laughing merrily beside me.

"Did you ever mention to your husband that you have a weakness for sea and open waters?" Daniel asked.

"Well, yeah!" I replied grinning. Today I just couldn't stop smiling.

"There is your answer then," he laughed loudly.

"Hey, Simi, is your husband coming?" Daniel asked her.

"No," she pouted. "Busy with work!"

"My girlfriend is also not here, mind being my date tonight?" he asked, offering her his arm.

She looked shocked, so he added, "Technically, it is like a tradition for the Maid of honour and Best man to hook up, but we both are loyal to our partners, so I promise I won't hit on you," he paused and Simi looked at me with terrified expressions. "And truth be told, being my date will save you from all the nasty proposals today," he laughed.

"Is he safe?" Simi asked me shamelessly in front of Daniel who raised his eyebrows.

"He is. He saved my relationship with Shaun, so I trust him," I replied.

"Date it is," Simi grinned and walked with Daniel, arm in arm.

♥

As we all boarded the ship, I was led to a separate section that was dedicated to me getting ready. Simi too got dressed there, along with my mother.

"Shaun is on the floor above us," Simi informed as she read through a chart that was placed in our room, "and the wedding will be in the middle of the ship, and reception is there as well."

I smiled as I looked out. The ship was moving now, and was heading towards the open seas.

"It is beautiful," I said.

The makeup girls arrived and started working on me. I could hear my mother and Simi talking in the next room while I got ready in isolation.

"I have never seen such a spectacular wedding," one of the girls spoke, "You are very lucky."

"I know, I am," I replied thinking what made this wedding so special. It was not the cruise or the ocean, but the love that we had for each other.

It took more than two hours for me to get ready and when I turned to see the mirror, I could not recognize myself.

Simi and my mother entered and gasped.

The gown I was wearing was simple yet elegant. It was fitting to my body, and had intricate floral work knitted on the border. My hair was half tied, and golden threads were woven in the braids that now were gracing my hair. The makeup was light but intense and it gave me a raw look. And the overall effect of everything combined was just unimaginable.

"Shaun is going to faint," Simi squealed.

"You look…" my mother paused, "beautiful."

"Thanks, mom," I smiled.

"I have to go," my mother added, "Simi will wait with you," and she turned and left while I stared after her sadly.

"I will go and talk to her," Simi huffed and left too.

I knew I had said I didn't care about what she said, but deep down her behaviour bothered me a lot. Not wanting to ruin my make up, I controlled my tears and decided to take a stroll on the deck of the ship.

I walked out and stood by the rails, staring at the horizon, while David and two more men stood close to me.

I was looking up ahead at the beautiful vision when my mother came to me.

"See… I told you he is not to be trusted," my mother spat as she pushed a newspaper in my hands.

Surprised, I looked down and saw an exposé of Shaun's affair with another girl with an intimate photo. I didn't even bother read it, but just pushed it back in her hands.

"You don't even want to know what he did with her?" my mother spat. "What is printed here?" she demanded.

"It is all in the past," I sighed.

"He spent twenty-four hours with her in a closed room… twenty-four hours Kaya… God knows what all he did with her… and there is more about their relationship in there," my mother's concern was etched on her face.

The words 'twenty-four hours in a closed room' bothered me, but I didn't show it in front of her.

"It is all in the past," I repeated.

"Kaya, men like him don't change. Who is to say you won't become his past too," she spoke, agitated.

"If that is my fate, then let it be... I will not ruin my present just because I fear what may come to pass," I spoke, trying very hard to control my tears.

"You are not the girl I raised, you are –" But what I was she didn't finish. She just turned and went away, leaving me alone with my miserable thoughts.

♥

David and my security tried to gain my attention, but I didn't turn. Finally, I felt, maybe finally my mother's words were getting to me.

"Kaya, what's wrong?" Shaun called from a distance.

I turned at the sound of his voice, he had his eyes covered with his hands – maybe because of the saying that seeing the bride before wedding was kind of bad luck.

"You spent the same twenty-four hours wrapped around her like you did with me?" I asked sombrely.

"What?" Shaun dropped his hands and gasped as his eyes widened with amazement. "You look wow... I mean... wow..."

Ignoring his expressions and words, I showed him the newspaper my mother had left behind.

He took it and glared at the content. "It was before you, everyone else was before you."

I just shook my head and turned my back to him. At this, he hugged me from behind and whispered, "You are the only one. Believe me, only one."

"Were you in a relationship with her before me?" I asked seriously.

"Yes, I was," he huffed.

"And you broke up with her," I asked.

"The day I saw you in that party," he informed.

"How do I know you won't break up with me?" I asked, my mother's words echoing in my head.

"And how do I know you won't fall out of love with me?" he asked.

"You seriously believe that?" I asked, shocked.

"And do you seriously believe I will leave you?" he asked in the same tone. "Look, future can be anything, but I know I won't stop fighting for you. I love you, you stupid stupid girl... so would you give us a chance?" he grabbed my face and insisted.

"Don't you think we have had enough trust issues recently to last us a lifetime?" he asked, as his gold flecked black eyes peered into mine.

I nodded and looked down and saw my beautiful white dress.

"I think our marriage is off to a rocky start," I sighed. "First, our mothers believe we are not marrying on the right time, now you have seen me in this dress before our wedding," I sobbed, "And –"

But before I could continue, he pulled my face and kissed me fiercely.

"You feel that?" he asked as he rubbed his nose against my cheekbone. "You feel the love and passion?" he asked, kissing me again.

"I do," I nodded.

"Till the time this love and passion is there, there is no rock in our journey. And by the way, you are looking just—" and he moaned in my ears, "Let's get this officially done so that I can make love to you as my wife."

And he dragged me back to my room, where the make-up girls started again on my face.

They worked on me for good thirty minutes where Simi continued to scold me non-stop. My mother was staring at me with a wild expression.

Knock! Knock!

Mia entered and she was looking divine. Wearing a navy-blue dress, she was looking nothing short of super-model.

"You look lovely," Mia smiled as she looked at me and for the first time, I didn't see a condescending look on her face. This lightened my mood slightly.

"I know this wedding is not a routine for your guys, but here, in our white weddings, we have a tradition," Mia smiled broadly. "We give the bride, *something old, something new, something borrowed and something blue.*" And she placed two small boxes on the table.

"Something old and something borrowed," she smiled as she opened the first box and showed me a small diamond studded bracelet. "This belonged to our grandma. She gave Shaun her ring, and me this bracelet," Mia spoke as she lifted my hand and caressed the ring Shaun had given me as a sign of love. She then placed the beautiful bracelet on my wrist and spoke, "I want it back, so it is 'borrowed', okay," she stressed and I nodded, tears fogging my eyes at her words.

"For something new and something blue," Mia hesitated as she looked at my mother, who was staring at us with mixed expressions, "Aunty, can you give us a minute?"

My mother narrowed her eyes but she didn't need telling twice. She turned and walked out.

"What is it?" Simi asked curiously.

And rolling her tongue in her cheek, Mia handed me a second package with the naughtiest expression. "Couldn't find anything better, so wear it inside."

I opened it and shrieked, "MIA!"

"Go on, and wear it," she practically pushed me in the bathroom. I didn't know what to do. "Don't make me come inside," Mia threatened.

Huffing and giggling at the same time, I pulled out a light blue G-string from the box and stared at it. It was nothing but a thin string of cloth and I was not even sure which side was front!

"Have you put it on?" Mia demanded from other side of the door.

"I am trying," I retorted as I started to pull down my pearl white panty from underneath my wedding gown.

"You know it is lucky for the bride to have all four!" Mia spoke as she barged inside, followed by Simi.

"Mia," I shouted, even Simi looked appalled. "Oh, you and I have same body parts," Mia rolled her eyes and she shoved the stringy blue piece in my hands. "Put it on!" she stressed and I obliged.

"It is uncomfortable," I complained as I put on my white underwear on top of it.

"Wait when your husband pulls it down with his teeth," Mia snickered and I blushed. Simi just stood there, unsure of whether to laugh or feel horrified that she was talking about her bother!

"I will see you outside then," Mia smiled, waved and left the room.

"The traditions are so different, aren't they?" Simi spoke as we made our way out finally. "We have things like '*mehndi, haldi'* and so on, and they have 'old, blue, new'."

"I am just glad we have someone who is willing to ensure we follow all traditions, irrespective of which culture we come from," I smiled.

Simi smiled with me and went ahead, while I waited around the corner for my father to join me.

A few minutes later, dad came and he drew a huge breath as he saw me in the wedding dress. I could tell he was not as mesmerized as a normal 'Non-Indian' father would have, but he was awe-struck enough.

"You look beautiful," my father spoke as I saw his eyes get misted.

"Thanks, dad," I smiled as I walked hand-in-hand with him to the centre of the ship, where the wedding ceremony was to take place.

Dad walked me down the aisle and this time my eyes didn't sway to anyone else and stayed glued to Shaun's super happy face. He was wearing a black tuxedo and though his attire was not much different than usual business days, his smile and happiness just made all the difference.

My dad placed my hand in his and he beamed with happiness.

"Dear friends and family members that all have gathered today," the minister started, "We are here to witness the bond that two beautiful souls share. With these rings," he lifted our wedding rings over his head, "you will be bound for life," and he handed one to Shaun…

"Kaya," Shaun sighed as he looked in my eyes, "I still remember the day I first saw you and even though it has been years, that memory is still fresh in my mind. You were so happy back then, and the smile you had in your eyes, the spark was priceless," he smiled. "Then I saw you last year again, and all my feelings for you, the ones that were stirred at the first sight came rushing back. My friends called it lust, but as I got to know you, I realized my feelings were never lust, they have always been of love. Love at first sight. Over the course of months, I have loved you, fought with you, cherished you and have spent endless hours with you, and all those moments have proven just one thing, I love you each day more. And as I look at you today, at your eyes, the smile you hold, the spark you have as you look at me, I feel my life has found its meaning. For I see you happier than before, and I now know I will be able to make you just as happy, if not more, than what you have made me. For I love you Kaya, and I will spend the rest of my life showing you and everyone who doubts me how much I truly, really, deeply love you."

Tears filled my eyes at his words and he placed a large solitaire studded ring on my finger.

"Kaya?" the minister pointed at me and I felt awkward. I didn't know!

"I have not prepared a vow," I started, "for I didn't know. But," I inhaled, "but I promise you this, that I will always love you. I will always cherish you. We both belong to such different worlds, so many people believe that I am making the worst mistake of my life by marrying you, but I don't think so. Because when I look at you, in your eyes, I don't see a billionaire brat who once held the reputation of a playboy. I don't see the man who is spoiled and stubborn...." He narrowed his eyes at these words, though his smile never ceased. "Well, you *are* spoiled and stubborn, there is no doubt about it," everyone laughed, and he huffed with a smile, "but it is a trait that makes you, you. When I look into your eyes, I see love. I see passion. I see a man who is honest and just. I see a man who would live miles away from his family just to ensure I am safe. A man who would move heaven and hell to see me smile. I don't need my entire life to know how much you love me, Shaun, I could see it in your eyes the day I met you. And though I have never told you this, I too fell in love with you even before that first introduction was over. As I stand in front of you, in a dress I never dreamed of wearing, I promise you one thing today - today I devote my life to you. I will spend the rest of my days showing you how much I love you, how much you mean to me, and to everyone in the world who think this is a mistake. I promise to love you so much that they will also say one day, this billionaire brat always does the right thing, be it work or be it life or be it his wife."

Shaun's face was alit with happiness as I placed the wedding band on his finger.

"With the power vested in me, I now pronounce you husband and wife," the minister spoke.

"You are killing me, you know that," Shaun muttered.

"You may kiss the bride," and with a breath-taking smile, Shaun bent down and kissed me with all his might, lifting me in his arms.

The whole deck was filled with applause, confetti, and balloons and as we broke apart, Daniel shouted, "And here is to Mrs and Mr Malani."

THE END.

ACKNOWLEDGEMENT

First and foremost, I thank all the beautiful readers. It is because of your love and motivation that I have written something entirely new and I hope you find it as good as my other works.

My special thanks to my beloved husband, ***Rajat Sharma***, for your love and evergreen support.

Big thanks and shout out to my wonderful kids, ***Vihaan*** and ***Vanya.*** You are so understanding and patient, and always allow me time to write and fuel my passion.

My lovely nephews, **Dwij** and **Aadit**, your cheery smile and sparkling eyes always light up my day.

To my parents, ***Dr. R. N. Gupta & Dr. Rekha Gupta, Justice Anil Sharma & Manju Sharma,*** for supporting me, motivating me, and making me what I am today.

My brothers and sisters, ***Anmol, Juhi, Shalabh, Kavita, Navendra, Harshita, Vipul, Arsh, Arushi and Arpita,*** thank you for being there for me at any time of the day.

My loving thanks to my friend, ***Shubham Sharma***, for your suggestions in this novel. Thank you for having endless discussions with me patiently, they have helped me make this book what it is today.

My big and special thanks to ***Anuj Kumar***, my publisher and a very good friend, for all your support and encouragement.

To my editor, ***Priyanka***, for your suggestions and support.

And last but not least, a big thanks to the almighty for guiding me, blessing me, and making me what I am today.

ABOUT KRITIKA SHARMA

Kritika Sharma is a proud mother of two beautiful children. She is also an author, blogger, reviewer and a dreamer. Besides her writing career, she is also a marketing professional with more than a decade of experience.

She loves to read, write, and cook Indian delicacies for her foodie husband. Her every waking second is dedicated to her family, and yet she finds time for her passion, i.e., her books.

She has published 10+ books across genres – Romance, Thriller, Non-Fiction etc. She loves to connect with her readers and is always available at

Email: kritikawrites@gmail.com

AuthorKritikaSharma

AuthorKritika

AuthorKritika

www.kritikasharma.in